RUSH JOBS

HOBSON & CHOI – CASE TWO

NICK BRYAN

ONE
MOVING DAY

"Choi! Great news! We're moving!"

"What?"

"To the old Social Awesome offices at the Inspiration Gestation Station!"

"Where?"

"Yeah, turns out they ain't using it now they're all dead."

"Don't you hate it there? Too trendy, too East London?"

"That wasn't me, must've been you. So if you could just sort out all the stuff from the old Peckham office and bring it over here? My mate Tony said he'd get his van over at nine."

"Who?"

"Thanks Choi. I'll buy you a sandwich if you're here by lunchtime."

"But... what?"

Angelina checked the time before clattering her phone aside again. Seven o'clock on a Monday? She'd planned on sleeping until eight, maybe texting Hobson to ask if they were open today after his nasty-looking leg injuries last week.

But not only was she reporting for duty at nine, she was a removal man. Did she have to wear low-slung trousers with her bum hanging out as well?

She stopped short of that, but found her most flexible jeans and a plain blue t-shirt – all still neatly hung up, of course. Despite living in her own personal loft conversion, she was still sixteen and that meant clean, ironed clothes appeared by magic.

Angelina told her Mum a few times that she really didn't need to iron knickers, pyjamas and cheap jeans, but that never stopped her. At least those lesser-seen ends of her arsenal would get an outing today.

Part of her frowned at turning up to her second week of work experience dressed like someone's Dad. Still, she pulled her hair back into a ponytail, put concealer on a particularly obvious spot and got on with it.

Adding flat shoes and a thick jacket, she thundered down the two flights of stairs from her isolation loft. As she hit the bottom, her mother emerged, bowl of cereal in hand. A huge smile sprang onto her face as she saw Angelina thump down in casual slacking gear. She was much better dressed herself, suited up and ready for a busy day working at the council.

She was tall and not-quite-thin – still, the height was the important part. Maximum intimidation, big hair.

Oh, and white as the driven snow. Angelina had known she was a more interesting colour for a long time, but still not worked out how she ended up in this family.

"Angelina! Are you staying home today? Is Mister Hobson still injured?"

This, Angelina felt, was not the supportive attitude they'd agreed on. Following a full week of nagging to drop this detective agency assistant gig, just because she was close to several bloody dog attacks, her Mum would have to do better than mere passive aggression.

"No, I'm going in, just dressed like this because we're moving offices. I'm supervising the packing," she added, puffing out her voice with authority.

"Oh. Well, at least that's a nice safe job, isn't it?" The smile stood firm. "How are you feeling about your last week of work experience?"

"My *second* week," Angelina said as she hefted a small bag onto her shoulder.

"Well, not that long to go, then you can have a nice summer waiting for your exam results."

"Okay. Can't wait." Her head shivered at the thought. She had to find a way to make Hobson let her stay, no matter what. Maybe she could bribe him with her meagre life savings.

"Absolutely." Her Mum clapped her hands. "Would you like a lift to the station?"

"I'm fine, thanks," Angelina said. "See you later."

"Did you want any breakfast? I made you this muesli."

She almost turned the whole meal down to make a statement, but stayed long enough to wolf down a cereal bar in the end. Left that bowl of cardboardy cereal to dry up and die though.

A few minutes after nine, Angelina sprinted out of Peckham Rye station, weaving around the annoying charity fundraisers who tried to engage her in conversation about suffering, and dashed down the road towards the office. She only stopped a few minutes at home to eat, but it cost her dearly when she missed the one train to get there on time.

She knocked at least two other commuters off their feet as she went, but they didn't hit their heads. Before she could be accosted by guards or passing do-gooders, she scrabbled off down the road, bag knocking against her leg. Thankfully, her stretchy clothes ducked and weaved well, but why did everyone walk so slowly around here?

A toddler darted out in front of her, singing, dancing and chuckling like a fool. Angelina lost her footing completely, cartwheeling off sideways into a pile of binbags. A cocktail of stinking brown goo dribbled out from the ripped plastic, leaking down her top and over her jacket. Some white jelly-blob latched onto her left shoe and refused to let go.

Angelina staggered to her feet, desperate to get clear of the mess. She scraped her feet on the floor, brushing yellow meat and blackening veg off her hair. A man emerged from the shop and started yelling in a strange language. Sounded like she'd wrecked his carefully arranged rubbish.

Hard not to feel nostalgic for last Thursday when she'd confronted a wide-eyed murderer. Shaking herself like a wet dog, she stomped around the final corner and squelched up to their building. The weather was just starting to get hot too, so the smell really had a chance to mature.

There was a plain white van out front, back doors wide open and a lanky, balding man in faded jeans and t-shirt sitting on the edge. Angelina almost ran back home when she realised how similar they were dressed. Piled up inside his van were a range of metal poles and scary sharp objects.

His eyes flicked up at the gooey sound of her approach. Once they'd focused in on her, he burst out laughing. Angelina collapsed against the wall until he'd finished.

Took a while. He was playing it right up, chuckling and rolling back where he sat.

At last, polite conversation started: "So, you're Choi? Hobson's new accomplice? Ain't you awfully young?"

"Angelina, sixteen years old," she said. "And you must be Tony?"

She extended a brown, sticky arm for a handshake. Tony gave a disdainful sniff and said: "Yeah, I ain't touchin' that."

"Oh, of course, sorry," she withdrew the hand, hoping her shame was hidden by filth. "Shall we get started on the move, then?"

"That's what I'm here for." He swept one arm towards the main door of the building. "Lead on, Angelina."

Keen to reach the building toilets and scrape herself clean, Angelina bounded up to the door of the Business Centre. She clicked it open with her entry card and strode into the tiny reception area – after a few days away, she'd forgotten quite how much it resembled a corridor with a desk rammed inside, brown, claustrophobic and clearly not fit for purpose. Then she jarred to a painful halt when Will sprang up from behind that very desk.

The hot receptionist slipped her mind too, even though she'd spent much of the last week fancying him and his trendy-without-trying-too-hard tall, fresh-faced looks. Even worse, he was wearing a decent shirt, tight trousers and having a good sweeping hair day, whereas Angelina looked like a homeless woman after a desperate bin dive.

"Hello." Will waved, after a moment. "Are you okay?"

"I'm fine. I tripped."

"I see. Do you need anything?"

"Can you sign Tony in while I clean myself up? He's here to help us move out."

"Yeah, I heard you were leaving, that's, um…" He got as far as leaning forward on his arms, before thinking better of it and sitting back. "Okay, you go get sorted, I'll deal with this."

"Thank you Will," Angelina said at high speed. She walked slowly to the next door, breaking into a scamper as soon as it closed.

After an hour moving stuff from the tiny office, Angelina was almost ready to phone her Mum and say: "You know what, that's it, you win."

Between awkward half-conversation with Hobson's friend Tony, total embarrassment in front of Will and stains which wouldn't shift, maybe she should cut her losses on this job.

The office itself was almost empty of Hobson's belongings now. All he had was paperwork, two elderly computers, four mouldy mugs and various office supplies. Most of the folders were so filthy or almost-empty, it didn't seem worth the energy of taking them downstairs.

Many rooms looked bigger when you pulled everything out of them, but no. Even with nothing but two desks, Hobson's old office was still a claustrophobic coffin. She kicked at a rock-solid grey-brown mark on the carpet, but only made it worse thanks to the disgusting state of her shoes.

She tried to feel some nostalgic sadness about leaving, but nothing came. Odd Hobson didn't want to come and say goodbye to the old place – wasn't he fond of it after however long?

Have to ask him later, assuming Tony didn't crash the van and Angelina didn't die of shame during her next trip through the foyer.

"Okay Lina, any last crap for the van?" Tony said, leaning into the small room from the corridor outside. "Hobson says the desks belong to the building, thank fuck. Carrying them down the stairs would be a total arsehole."

Apparently she was 'Lina' now. Should've let Tony call her 'Choi'.

Rather than protesting, she shook her head and closed the door on the old office.

After all the build-up in her mind, their final exit from the Brightman Business Centre wasn't too bad. She got as far as passing Will's desk, when he said: "Well, see you then."

"Bye," she waved and smiled, "thanks for, you know, everything."

"No worries. Hope you enjoyed your week here."

"Um, yeah, it was amazing, I really…"

Just as they almost started up a talk, of course, Tony leaned through the glass doors and yelled: *"Oi! Lina! Come on! This bloke dressed as a pimp is giving me weird looks!"*

Will let out an involuntary chuckle. "Do they call you Lina?"

"Um, he does."

"Okay then. Bye, Lina. Come back some time, but have a shower first."

Angelina found she didn't mind as much when Will did it. At long last, she fled the building before anything else could go wrong and leapt into the passenger seat of Tony's van.

The unsettling local character known as 'The Pimp' was indeed there by the roadside, giving them a long, furious glare as they pulled away. He was wearing a garish red suit and huge tall matching hat as ever – he *must* own more than one – and grinning.

Desperate for a distraction from Tony's crunchy driving and that weirdo outside, Angelina grabbed her mobile and called the boss.

"Hobson? We're on the way."

"Thanks, Choi. Got any spare clothes to change into? Tony texted to say you smell like shit."

"No, just the ones I'm wearing. I could head home?"

"No worries, just don't stink out the new place too much. I got a client coming in soon and they're already quite upset."

"Oh, what's the case?"

"Missing persons. Her sister went bye-bye."

"Wow, that's cool."

"Don't say *that* to her either. And start keeping spare clothes at the office, you're always getting covered in blood or rotten shit in this job."

"I'll *definitely* pass that on to my mother."

"What?"

"Nothing. Back soon!"

Before Tony's van fully stopped, Angelina leapt from the passenger door and dashed across the car park, drawing wrinkled noses from passing trendy cardigan workers. She hurled her entire body flat against the glass front of the Inspiration Gestation Station and pounded at the pane. After several frenzied seconds, a wide-eyed Jacq flicked the button to release it.

The poor receptionist was such a fuzzy-cardigan-wearing, relaxed little dream girl, she always seemed unprepared for any stress. Her hair hung in curls, eyes forever wide.

Like a dog released from a trap, Angelina tore through up to Jacq's desk, leaning over until she recoiled. Her feet crunched into the astroturfed floor, leaving brown stains in their wake. The stark colours on the walls were almost insulting to her right then.

"Jacq!" Angelina yelled. *"Do you have a shower here?"*

"Um, yes. First floor," she quailed, pointing towards the lift with a shaking hand.

Angelina pushed off towards the flower-painted lift doors. She was so desperate to get clean, even the mutilated corpse she'd once seen from this room didn't occur to her.

The lift closed, and Angelina disappeared up into the IGS. Lifts *and* a shower. She could already tell she was going to like working here.

TWO
NEW TERRITORY

Only the first day, and Hobson was already sick to his fucking stomach of working here.

This new super-cool modern building insisted on a public directory of companies renting – apparently proper office blocks did that sort of thing. Because he'd wanted to take on the offices of Social Awesome ASAP, he retained their phone number. As soon as word of his move got out – thanks to bloody Twitter, it was more or less instantaneous – the phone started ringing.

He unplugged it after a handful of disturbances, obviously. The few he'd answered were all journalists asking about the events of last week: his fight with the wolf, how he'd solved the mystery, what his involvement with the case was – questions with answers either too secret or too embarrassing.

A couple of new neighbours popped in to say hello, but he barely acknowledged them. Maybe he should make nice with these people, but Hobson couldn't be arsed. He'd send Choi round to placate the wankers once she'd finished moving his stuff over.

On that thought, the lift rumbled open; a moment later, so did the door to his office. A large box shoved its way through.

Hobson himself reclined at the old reception desk in the middle of the room, surrounded by a ghost town of dead computers. He flipped through the latest in a string of files plucked from Edward Lyne's office, feet up.

"Just leave it over there, Choi," he said, pointing without looking. "We'll sort everything out this afternoon."

"I'm not your damn intern, Johnny," the box said, and Hobson finally looked up.

"Oh, alright Tony? Where's Choi?"

"Little Lina ran off for the shower as soon as we got here. She wasn't much use at the fetching and carrying anyway, and the smell was rank. I'm gonna need a fucktonne of air fresheners for the front of my van."

"There's a shower in this building? It's like I've died and gone to hippie hell."

Tony dropped his box. "Tell me about it. What're you *doing* here?"

"Getting involved. This is where the business is." Another phone rang, pinging out a different, harsher tone from the one he'd unplugged. "Speaking of which, internal line."

He seized the receiver. "Hi Jacq, what is it?"

"Mister Hobson, Michelle Carlton is here to see you."

"Send her up, cheers very much."

He hung up, leapt to his feet, the thought of *getting back to work* rushing to his head. Pacing around, he clasped his hands behind him. "Okay Tony, could you finish moving the stuff up? Don't mean to be a twat, but I gotta talk to this woman. Sort some money out for you later."

"No worries, Johnny." Tony threw a wave over his shoulder and went for the exit.

Hobson ran a quick hand through his hair. Taking one last look around the mid-move mess, he wondered if it was too late to find a cupboard to shove it in.

Apparently so, as the lift doors were already humming open. A tall, brunette woman emerged, Tony slipping in behind her to head down. Hobson could only just see his new client through the windows embedded in the office door between then. He stared for a few moments, until she took a deep breath and pushed through.

Determined to pick this up smoothly, Hobson indicated towards Edward Lyne's old corner office. "Ms Carlton, nice to see you. Shall we talk in there?"

When Hobson called Michelle Carlton to set up this appointment, she'd sounded relieved and weepy. That awkward, stilted conversation left him wondering whether she'd turn up a broken woman or put a brave face on it.

It was the latter. She'd worn a sleek blue dress, made enough effort with make-up for him to notice it. He felt even worse about the awful state the office was in. Was this his new class of clientele? Attractive, well-dressed young ladies? Would he need to buy an even more expensive plain black suit?

Should probably at least have put away some of these piles of half-read files which already covered his workspace.

Hobson turned sharply around his desk, gesturing towards the chair he'd pulled in front of it earlier.

There hadn't been one there before, Edward Lyne clearly never wanted anyone to get too comfortable, but Hobson's clients usually needed to talk for at least a few minutes.

She sank gracefully into the seat, folding her legs artfully as she went. Hobson tried his best not to just thump into his own, but it was inevitable in the end. There was no window, so he turned the light on, even though the yellow glow wasn't flattering for either of them.

"Okay, so, Ms Carlton, shall we get right into this?"

"Yes, of course," she said, leaning forward. "It's about my sister, Jo."

"Short for Josephine?"

"Joanne."

"Uh-huh," Hobson said, scribbling down notes on a pad. He couldn't type fast enough to do this on a computer. "And she's gone missing?"

"Yes. Two days or so ago, she vanished on the way home from work."

"Work. Uh-huh, and where's that?"

"The Anderson's supermarket in Hackney, the big one, she was assistant manager."

"The big evil supermarket chain, gotcha. And someone saw her leave?"

"Yes," Michelle said, breath rushing, "I saw the security tape. She leaves the building, but never makes it back. No-one seems to have seen a thing."

"Cops not done anything?"

"They've asked around, her picture's posted online, but nothing yet, and I know it's important to act quickly."

"Right."

"So I thought I'd get you involved too after I saw you on the news dealing with that murder. You solved it in only four days, after all."

"Well, y'know," Hobson said. "It felt longer."

"But you did fight a wolf! I thought, you know, that's someone I want looking for Jo. Someone who won't give up, no matter what."

"Thanks," Hobson said, grinning, "I'm not a superhero though. I put my socks on one at a time, just like everyone else."

"I'm just so happy you agreed to meet me at all, Mister Hobson. You must have so many cases coming in."

That gave Hobson pause. Was he a celebrity? Was this woman dressing up and flattering him because he was famous? Weird as fuck, but he couldn't let it break his flow.

"A few, yeah. So was Jo alright, is there any reason she'd want to, y'know, vanish?"

"No," she said firmly, "she'd just moved in with two friends, she was happy."

"Right. Good. I've just got a few more specific questions about her disappearance and then I'll get started, okay?"

Angelina entered her new office, still rubbing her wet hair with paper towels from the bathroom. There, she saw a tall woman in a long, shiny blue dress emerging from Hobson's side-office. It was hard not to feel slobby in comparison – Angelina might be clean underneath now, but her faded clothes were still lazy and stained.

She did a small wave and went to the other side of the room, mindful of Hobson's earlier warning not to scare clients with the smell. Tony sat at Emily's old desk, reading the paper next to a pile of boxes.

"Afternoon, Lina," he said, not looking up. "Finally had that shower?"

"Yes, thank you."

"About time."

She stuck her tongue out at him as Hobson escorted the client away. He kept himself visible at the door until she'd entered the lift and disappeared. After a lingering pause, he came over to deal with the other two.

"Tony," he said, rifling through his wallet, "here's thirty quid for your petrol and time, that alright?"

"Yeah, thanks Johnny." Tony seized the two notes and counted them pointlessly.

"Good. You can head off now, thanks for everything. See you for a pint sometime."

You didn't need to tell Tony twice, he'd yelled his thanks and left before Hobson even finished speaking. Considering they had a lovely new office and a fresh case, Angelina thought, her boss looked a bit grumpy.

"Right, Choi, new case: that woman's sister Jo is missing."

"Wow."

"I know. You get sandwiches, I'm making some calls. After that, you can pile up all Social Awesome's shit in one corner and roll out our stuff around the place."

"Okay. That really won't take long, our old office was a cupboard compared to this one."

"Good, thanks. And at around five, I'm going to need you to send a tweet announcing we're looking into this case."

"A tweet?" Angelina gasped, her jaw dropping open without dignity.

"Yes, a tweet, saying we're on this and we're visiting her old workplace in the morning. That a problem?"

"No, it's just... you *want* me to tweet?"

"Believe me, Choi, I'm much less happy about it than you, but I'm hoping it'll shake a few branches loose. Let's get on with this, yeah?"

THREE
HIT THE SHOPS

It was eight o'clock on Tuesday morning in Hackney. Other commuters were still lumbering into the station, blinking in the too-early sunlight. Angelina picked her way out between them.

Already on the second day of her maybe-final week in work experience, after spending most of Monday lugging boxes. What if last week's furry murder case was a freak one-off? Did regular employment at Hobson's agency consist of sending tweets and unpacking dirty coffee mugs?

Even so: she needed to prove her importance to the company before the end. Otherwise, it was back to her boring house, forced to get a job at McDonalds like all the other kids.

Last night at home was torture – her Mum practically crowing with victory over the fact her poor daughter had a dull day. Even when Angelina tried to let her know they were working on a missing persons case, it seemed to go straight through her.

Too busy telling her husband, in a gleeful sped up voice, that the work experience placement would be over soon, thank goodness, and if she still wanted a job, Angelina could shelve books at the library. Even if it was grounded in a desire to protect her, couldn't the woman recognise her adoptive daughter's misery?

Well, at least they were out of the office now, on the move again, on the trail of missing Jo Carlton. Picking up the pace, she passed more small shops and brightly coloured, blocky cafés. The tables were beaten-down relics from a second hand shop, prices terrifying.

The sun was out, a gentle Spring warmth beginning to rise around her. Corner grocery shops were open, selling small items to passing commuters, all full to bursting. She soon worked out why.

The last bank of regular-sized retail units dropped away, to reveal the massive Anderson's supermarket. A huge brick block demanding empty space around it to insulate other buildings from its majesty, trolleys and cars scattered around like worshippers surrounding a temple. The windows were dark, shutters down, all closed for business. Angelina shivered at seeing a store so massive shut in daylight, as if she'd turned the corner into the apocalypse.

Across the road from Anderson's was Subway, where she was meeting Hobson. He perched on a stool at the window, facing out over the street. His eyes followed her for a moment as she made for the door, then went back to staring at the supermarket.

He was taking huge bites out of a sticky mass of bread and ketchup. Angelina hoisted herself onto the smooth plastic seat next to him and retched slightly.

"Morning, Hobson."

"Choi."

"Those breakfast sub things are foul. Is that a fried egg shoved in there?"

"Damn right. Want one?"

"No, I'm good."

"No breakfast for you, then." Hobson squelched his sandwich down onto its greaseproof paper, making Angelina recoil. He pointed across the road: "This, in case you ain't guessed, is the supermarket where Jo Carlton worked. I've been watching it for an hour."

"Yeah, why are people hanging around outside like that?"

"Because, Choi," he said, mouth full, "it was meant to open at seven, but not a peep."

"Why?"

"Because of your stupid tweet. We announced we're looking into it and they ran for cover."

"I don't get it," Angelina said. "The picture of Jo's been online for days, the police are looking for her, but we tweet about it once and they shut up shop?"

"I know, pretty good, eh?"

"I still don't understand, though."

"I have some history with these guys, they're more worried about me than the law. Come on." He shoved the last fragment of sandwich into his mouth and hopped down from his stool, rushing all of a sudden. "Let's get in their faces."

A nervous tremor grew in Angelina's stomach, but she needed to prove herself a useful and obedient helper in this final week. She slid from her stool and followed him out of Subway.

As he reached the edge of Anderson's car park, Hobson hesitated before putting his foot on the tarmac. It was stupid, of course – no one was home, they ran away at the mere prospect of him turning up. He had the upper hand.

He kept moving with only a small break in his stride, easy to blame on his painkiller-dulled injuries from that wolf attack. Choi probably didn't notice.

The morning was still crisp and cold, not many people out doing weekly shopping yet. A few confused-looking patrons still gathered at the entrance to Anderson's, as if they knew it must be a mistake. A supermarket closed during opening hours was an aberration. Soon enough, the natural order would reassert itself.

As Hobson stepped under the scaffolded glass canopy that protected the front door, all eyes were on him. A pale guy in a ratty jumper, several suburban men and women carrying expensive everlasting carrier bags, no doubt thought they were clever coming out this early for their shopping. Tangible hope floated in the air that he was a corporate rep come to end their suffering.

Most gazes slid off when they didn't see the familiar light-blue Anderson's uniform, but a couple lingered.

"You're John Hobson!" said one woman, a couple of others echoed her. "Yeah, the guy who fought the wolf."

"Yup," he said. "That's me."

"Are you here to investigate why Anderson's ain't open?" The next man sounded out of breath with excitement.

"Yeah. Exactly. I care about your fuckin' shopping experience."

RUSH JOBS

Suddenly, a commotion. A spatter of footsteps behind a low bass rumble, and everyone outside Anderson's turned towards the noise. At this time of the morning in London, any fast movement was anathema, snapping people out of their mid-commute haze.

But at the outskirts of the car park, a group of people were bucking the trend, leaping the tiny walls, skirting the few cars and dashing towards the mighty brick fortress at the centre.

When they reached visible distance, it was obvious they all had hoodies pulled down low over their faces in a range of colours – green, red, grey. Choi gasped, pulling in closer to Hobson as if she thought they were about to mug her.

"Choi," he muttered, "you gotta stop judging people just 'cos of how they dress."

There were four of them, jeans stained and yelling. The noise, the most intimidating part of the approach, skittered from the wheels of a clattering shopping trolley, rattled around the walls by one of the skinnier kids. He charged it towards the shop, head bent low over the plastic handlebar to reduce drag, square metal frame crashing and swerving from pressure on the wheels. Most of the hopeful customers ran screaming.

Hobson stood firm though, waiting as the invaders dashed up to a huge window halfway along the front wall. The deep rumble of the trolley wheels felt like a riot in his gut.

The rest hung back while one of the larger boys reached into their cart and hefted out the one object inside – a heavy sledge hammer. He needed both arms to wield it, straining but never struggling.

Stopping only to make sure his hoodie was tight over his head, the big kid drew the business end back and swung it hard into the glass.

Impressively, the double glazing withstood one blow, only a small pattern of initial cracking. But its attacker just brought the hammer down again harder.

This time, the pane smashed into tiny pieces, falling out of the frame like rain. They bounced off the hoodies, sending all remaining civilians except the thin, pale bloke running away.

The shattered glass cascaded, sprinkling off the rows of chained up trolleys, sparkled in the morning sunshine. Hobson couldn't help but grin at the sight of it. Choi tried to run away, but he grabbed her entire forearm tightly in one hand.

"Choi. It's alright, they won't hurt us."

Sure enough, the raiding party never looked twice at the general public. Just scrambled through the empty window-frame as quick as they could. The hammer-wielder used the side of his weapon to scrape stray shards off the bottom, although all his mates wore gloves anyway. Then he dropped the thing in the trolley with a clang and left it, running after the rest.

After a tiny pause, the thin, sickly-looking guy near Hobson and Choi ran to leap into the shop as well. Couldn't blame him for taking a chance, looked like he hadn't eaten in months. An alarm started wailing through the empty space.

"So, I reckon we've got about ten minutes to search the premises, you game?" Still holding Choi's arm, Hobson nodded towards Anderson's.

"I... you... you knew?" she said, taking in his utter calm.

"Gave them twenty quid each, promised them the shop was empty."

"I…"

"C'mon, Choi." Hobson grinned. "You *know* my police ex will let us off if we get arrested, so let's get in there. Don't be boring."

He released his grip on her wrist. She snatched it away and stood, motionless for a moment, before nodding. They clambered into the empty supermarket together, sirens sounding in the far distance already.

By the time Angelina lowered herself down onto the dusty supermarket floor, Hobson was already halfway across the row of checkouts. She scrambled around the thin *'Closed'* barriers in her way, breathing heavily just to catch up. Shouts echoed around the empty store.

Up in front of her, aisle after aisle of domestic products. So much stuff that even if she were here to steal, she wouldn't know where to start. DVDs? Chocolate? Toilet roll? Buckets? Gardening gloves?

Looking over her shoulder, one of the kids was already running towards the broken window, arms full of video games. The alarm was even more deafening inside the building. No soothing background pop music playing right now, just a vague electronic hum below the wails and shouts.

"C'mon!" Hobson pointed across the front of the shop, shouting to be heard. "Let's keep the fuck away from the electronics section. That's where the kids will concentrate. Maximum value for resale, and they just like that shit."

Angelina nodded, trying to look like she smashed and grabbed all the time. If this outing got back to her

Mum, no arguing or guilt-tripping would get her out of the house ever again. Although still better than the police offering her a similar arrangement, with more metal bars and scheduled exercise.

She didn't say anything – just padded along behind Hobson, hoping not to attract any attention. They turned into the groceries aisles, a modern garden of green plastic crates. None of the kids were there, but the pale guy from outside was filling a stolen bag-for-life up with fruit. He was all skin and bones, Angelina thought – homeless, surely.

She stopped to stare, whilst Hobson strode up the aisle towards the back of the shop. Eventually, the maybe-homeless man looked up from throwing apples into his shopping. Stared right at her.

Angelina was rooted to the spot. His eyes looked off-colour, hair close to dying on his head.

"Choi, for fuck's sake," Hobson snapped. "He's not a work of modern wanky art. Snap out of it, we've got a job to do."

She jumped, blinked and dashed along. As they passed the thin man, she heard Hobson say: "Oh, make sure you take some canned food and an opener, yeah? That fresh shit will just go rotten."

He muttered a reply, too quiet to make out, as the two of them shivered up the chilled aisle. Just as they turned along the back, one of the kids in hoodies dashed around straight into their path. Angelina tensed up instantly, feeling Hobson do the same.

The boy paused for a second. "Just want some cheese, yeah? All good?"

"Yeah, fine," Hobson said, moving on again. Angelina saw the kid's face slip out from under the hood as he reached down. Guilty, the first thing she registered was that he was black, also that he looked well enough fed.

At the back, a pair of swing doors away from the shop floor. They were not well locked, flying open with two kicks from Hobson's boot. Suddenly, as if it was nothing special at all, they were backstage at the supermarket. Hobson didn't seem impressed, but Angelina felt like she was watching a DVD special feature.

They emerged into a huge, open passage that rolled down to the warehouses. To the left was an office marked *MANAGER* in heavy, permanent letters. Glass walls so he could watch people. Across the way was another transparency-enclosed room, full of messy tables and lockers. There was a microwave, chunky furniture in bland colours, dozens of soup-stains badly cleaned up – must be the staff room. Toilets nearby.

The whole place was shrouded with depressing darkness, even after the lights sputtered into life automatically. Back here, the alarm was even shriller, screaming out from a speaker directly above them.

Hobson was already on his way into the manager's office, opening it up with another kick. Not wanting to be left alone, she scurried after him.

"Hobson, why are we here?"

"Mm, well." He flicked open the top of a filing cabinet and started rifling through papers, shoved it closed and moved to the next drawer. "We're here to search this office quickly, so get on with it. Looking for pay records. I wanna know how they got their workers."

"You mean like a recruitment agency?"

"Yes!" Hobson snapped his fingers. "Exactly like that. Didn't think you'd know what they were."

"I'm not a baby, you know," she said, reaching down to flick through the documents left on the desk. He either ignored her or didn't hear over the scream of the alarm.

They found stock details, bills, letters, assessments, items of paperwork Angelina didn't recognise, but nothing detailing staff or wages. Hobson was almost at the bottom of the filing cabinet already, slamming the penultimate drawer with a particularly irritable swearword.

As she took another step around the desk to reach the other end, her foot slipped on something, losing traction for a moment. She reached down, underneath the near side of the desk, and tugged out a small rectangle of paper out.

It looked a lot like a payslip. She waved it in the air. "Hobson! Is this the sort of thing?"

He was up from his squat in a flash, plucking it from her hand without so much as a polite word. Still, the grin spreading across his face said it all.

"Perfect. Good work, Choi. Where was it hidden?"

"Um, on the floor," she said, blushing.

"Ha. Guy must've dropped it disposing of everything else. Told you I'd panicked them. Alright."

"So," Angelina said, trying to keep in the loop, "what does it say?"

"Apparently they source all their staff from Rush Recruitment, exactly what I thought. Now, let's get the hell out of here before the coppers show up."

"I thought your ex-wife would let you off anyway."

"Never hurts to avoid getting caught. Don't overmilk the favours, Choi. Makes it easier when you *need* them."

He swept out of the manager's office and back up the hallway, shoving the doors open again. She ran along behind him as ever, half-expecting to see a devastated retail landscape ravaged by hoodies with hammers. But once her eyes squinted through the sudden light, everything was as they'd left it. The alarm kept clanging, homeless man disappeared. Without incident, they paced back towards the front. More urgency in Hobson's step though, as sirens drew closer.

Soon, they were clambering out of the front window, ready to make their escape with police nowhere in sight. The gang of kids out front prepared to roll away their trolley, full of electronics, DVDs, booze and blocks of cheese. Good haul, she had to admit.

And it was all over. Everything was fine. Air rushing back into her body, Angelina pulled out her phone to check her Mum hadn't seen this on the news and texted a burst of indignant middle class fury.

A second later, the cheese kid from earlier snatched the mobile from her hand. *"Hey!"* She yelled out, waving her hands impotently in its wake.

Hobson was a few steps away, but turned instantly and stormed back. The boy's mouth turned down, started to burble noises. Definitely realised he'd been stupid.

He never got to apologise, though. Instead, Hobson grabbed his forearm, using his other hand to snatch her phone back, then clench it inside his fist and punch the thief cleanly in the face. The hood slumped off his head to show a nose already beginning to pump out blood, eyes staring with shock and a childlike sense of betrayal. Angelina couldn't stop shaking.

"Anyone else?" Hobson looked over towards the others, as he lifted the misbehaving child up by that one arm.

They didn't seem up for it. Just turned their trolley on its wheels and raced away. A couple looked back, concern for their friend registering. Still, it never outweighed the need to get out of there before either Hobson or the police got them.

"You alright, Choi?"

She nodded, as her whole body trembled.

"Good. Let's get the fuck out of here."

He gripped the kid's belt with his other hand, hefted the weight for a second, before tossing him through the empty window. He crunched against a checkout desk and tumbled to the floor, eyes unfocused. Only then did Hobson hand Angelina back her phone, blood smeared across the fake-leather red case.

FOUR
DISTURBED DUO

"Hi, this is Rush Recruitment, for when you need staff NOW! No-one's in to take your call at the moment, but leave a message after the beep and we'll get back to you ASAP!"

Beep.

"Yeah, this is John Hobson. I've called you three times now. I know you're in fucking hiding or whatever, but could you ring me back please? I'm pretty sure you're involved in this Jo Carlton case, and it'd make all our lives easier if you'd co-operate like good boys, okay? Thanks, bye."

After hanging up his mobile and glaring at the stack of papers on his desk, Hobson leaned back and rubbed his fingers deep into his eyes. Just hearing Rush's answerphone message was causing flickers in his memory. An endless line of horrible conversations in quiet rooms, leading to worse exchanges in loud ones.

He'd smashed his fist into that stupid kid's face earlier, maybe that started him remembering. Or perhaps hearing their name would've done the job either way, who the fuck knows? His hands shook without permission.

There was a reason he didn't do this stuff anymore. He should've left well alone. A yell clambered up his throat, he converted it into a growl just in time. A layer of sweat collected under his shirt.

He'd sorted one difficult case without needless violence last week, he told himself. Well, some injury to his lower leg, but that was healing. He could do it again. He already had a good idea what happened, so it should be easy. Find Jo Carlton for her sister, collect the money, move on.

Maybe see if Michelle Carlton fancied a drink some time, but that was a secondary goal.

Choi believed he could do it, after all. He spotted her leaning back in her chair to get a visual on Hobson, no doubt curious about that low roaring noise. He'd opted to take over Edward Lyne's old personal space, the only desk here with its own walls and door, because he was the boss.

It was full of old furniture, devoid of natural light. Perfectly serviceable, but right now he hated it for not being his old, comfortable desk back in the longstanding Peckham office.

He shot Choi a burst of eye contact and she whipped back round to face the workspace she'd settled at – Lettie Vole's old receptionist spot, near the front door.

With a grunt of bored irritation, he let Edward Lyne's expensive chair clunk back into the upright position and stood up. Another noise escaped him from the exertion. Hobson was getting old.

"Choi," he said, emerging into the larger communal space. "Any luck?"

"Um, no, sorry," she said, babbling. "Been calling the store manager's house but he's not answering. No answerphone either so I can't even leave a message."

"Fuck. Do we have a mobile number yet?"

"No," she said, obviously panicking. "Googling for it."

"Right. Anything else?"

"Um, a few journalists calling to ask if we've made any progress on the Carlton case yet…"

"Fuck's sake."

"Well, we did tweet that we were working on it, so it's kinda our fault, I supp…"

"Choi, shut the fuck up," he snapped, "it's not like…"

Mumbling an apology, Hobson disappeared back to his own walled-off office, this time shutting the door behind him. He lay back in his seat, staring at his pile of inherited paperwork.

Picked up the file with *JOHN HOBSON* across the front and flicked open to another random page. This time, he lasted nearly three minutes before slamming it shut.

Need to get through it at some point. Gotta work out why the fuck Lyne had it, who they were to each other. Instead, he was picking at an even less advisable thread of his history via this kidnapping case.

Maybe fucking later. He called Rush Recruitment for the fourth time, only to get their voicemail yet again. Breathing deeply, Hobson talked himself down from throwing his phone against the wall.

All Angelina had to help get hold of the supermarket manager was his name and a brief TV news interview about what a nice person Jo Carlton once was. Based on that evidence, Gregory James was another aging white man. Overweight, balding and sputtering pleasantries.

"She was such a good girl, yes," he'd muttered. *Good girl?* Angelina wasn't sure she'd tolerate anyone calling her that, and she wasn't even a legal adult yet.

Unfortunately, Mister James wasn't taking his duty to keep her occupied seriously. Even when she found a number, he wouldn't answer the phone, or even turn on his machine to let her leave a message. Hobson said they just wanted to talk to him. Find out how he got involved with Rush Recruitment and what he knew about Jo Carlton's disappearance.

She could handle that – it sounded like what they'd been doing last week, without any risk of unfamiliar people or violence. Unlike Hobson hurling that kid through the window. According to the internet, the boy got the blame for the entire break-in, and she didn't quite get why or how. Was Ellie intervening again? Or were they scapegoating the black hoodie kid because he was there, assuming any mention of an older guy paying him was a lie?

She buried her head in her palms. Maybe the world of crime was dangerous and she'd be better off in a regular office or back at school. God knows her Mum already texted to check she was "staying safe", whatever that meant.

The door to Hobson's office floated open yet again, and she looked up with cautious hope. He stalked out of the office, coat already on and shoulders low.

"C'mon Choi, enough of this bullshit. We're going round to Gregory whatsit's house to get some truth."

She leapt up and pulled her coat off the back of her seat. "Sure! So, um, you think he'll speak to us?"

"What?"

"Well, he doesn't seem to be picking up the phone."

"And if he doesn't open the door either, I'll knock it down and threaten him until he fucking talks." There wasn't a smile with that. "Enough shitting around."

"Right." The spike of excitement in her gut sank to a flat tickle. "Okay."

Gregory James lived in the suburbs, with no car or wife, but a bigger house than many who did have those things. Hobson sat in a bus shelter across the road, Choi alongside, glowering at the well-maintained brick terrace, waiting to see if he'd save them the trouble of knocking.

Neither had spoken for a while. A building rain fell around them, three buses passed. Each slowed to see if the grumpy detectives were interested in boarding, before accelerating into the distance.

Choi tried to make conversation, but after she met only annoyed grunts, gave up and started checking her phone. Next, she took to announcing facts about the case whenever she scrolled by them on Twitter. Despite his desire for peaceful sulking, these were sometimes useful, so he granted nods and mumbled approval.

Better than the time she showed him a picture of some cat – not even her own damn pet – and he'd stared at her until she backed away.

The last time she held up the phone, a short video extract played. It was jerky as shit, but he recognised

Michelle Carlton's sad, pretty face. She still wore the same dress as yesterday – must've been one of her best, Hobson thought.

"We beg Jo to come home if she can hear us," she cried, "and if the gang who attacked the supermarket have made threats, the police will protect her."

Michelle rubbed her eye, letting out the sob she'd been keeping in throughout their meeting at the IGS. She would cry in front of the cameras, but not John Hobson, celebrity detective.

His ex-wife Ellie, the detective-sergeant, sat next to Michelle in a steely grey suit. She glanced into the camera – straight at Hobson, as if she knew he was watching. Her hard eyes came alive for a second, before the two-minute long extract clunked to a stop. A veil of ads fell across the screen of Choi's mobile.

"Are you alright, Hobson?" Choi said.

"Yeah. No. Yeah. Don't know."

"Okay." She looked back down at her phone.

Hobson looked across the street at Gregory James' house and saw a whisper of movement at the upstairs window. Choi saw it too, but before he could usher them across the road to tackle the target, she turned to him, looking weirdly calm and adult.

"Hobson," she began, without a stammer, "who *are* Rush Recruitment? I mean," small laugh, "I assume they aren't a real temp agency?"

He considered brushing past her, but started talking instead. His voice felt like it was being worked remotely by some puppet master. "I used to work for them, a few years ago."

"So you worked in recruitment?"

"I… no. I was more at the muscle end. They're bad arseholes, Choi."

"What *do* they do, then?" she demanded.

"Smuggling. People and goods, but mostly people."

"Right. Why'd you quit?"

"My wife left me. Would've been better to get out before it came to that, but better late than never, you know?"

"I suppose so. So that's why we took the case?"

"Um, Edward Lyne had a file on me, possibly from them. When Jo Carlton happened just after I found that, I didn't think it could be a coincidence. Wanted to get out in front of them."

"Is that a good idea?"

"I dunno."

She kept staring at him. Well, he'd expected worse from that revelation. Now, though, he really was twitching and ready to crack on.

"Okay Choi. We alright?"

"Yeah."

She didn't look entirely sure about that, but it'd have to do.

"Ready to go have a word with Mister Supermarket Manager?"

Face still pale, she nodded.

A mist of feelings swirled around Angelina's head as she and Hobson stepped out of the bus shelter and across the road. The pounding rain wasn't helping her grim state of mind. It poured around her umbrella, splashing back into her legs every few seconds. Bloody hell, it was *late May*.

When would the sunshine start?

They slipped between the brick towers that separated the house from the street. After crossing the small front garden in a few steps, Hobson rapped on the door with his knuckles.

Waited around ten seconds, punched it with his fist.

"Mr James! Come on!" So far, he sounded more bored than angry. "Open up. I don't want this to turn nasty, but I'm not going anywhere until we've spoken to you."

No response. She gulped and looked up at the house. No twitching curtains, no snatched glances, just a tower of brick and window.

Not bothering with another smack, Hobson waved Angelina away. Bracing himself against the doorframe with both hands, he lifted up his foot for a kick. The door looked heavy-duty, but so were Hobson's boots.

Before she could see who would win, a weedy shout of "Wait wait wait wait *stop I'm coming!*" emerged from inside.

Looking like he'd been cut off in the middle of an important speech, Hobson lowered his foot as the locks crunched off the door. It swung open, revealing the exact useless, terrified man Angelina expected. Trembling, large, hair thinning despite not being *that* old, long worried face like some cartoon character. Loosened shirt collar, like a banker who'd just been fired.

"Mister James," Hobson said, "nice of you to speak to us. Can we have a word?"

"Whatever you want, just don't hurt me, please."

Gregory James trembled up at Hobson as if he were a giant. The guy wasn't even particularly short, but he backpedalled across his own hallway.

"Okay, come on, we're not gonna beat you up, we just want to ask some questions."

Thanks to Hobson's size and gruff tone, even that sounded scary. Gregory James took more quick paces back. In the end, he tripped over his own stairs and plopped down onto his good-sized bottom.

"What do you want to know? I'll tell you anything, please don't hurt me, what do you want?"

"Oh Jesus." Hobson turned back to Angelina. "If *this* was the guy clearing out the evidence from the manager's office, no wonder he dropped a payslip."

A short pause, interrupted only by the audible chattering of Gregory James' teeth.

"Look, we just want to ask about Rush Recruitment," Hobson said.

"Oh God, I swear I just employed the people from them, I never knew.... Oh God…"

"I'm sure."

More trembling.

"Fuck this." Hobson stepped further inside the doorway to let Angelina enter. "Choi, talk to this man and find out what he knows about Rush Recruitment and Jo Carlton."

"Me?"

"I'm concerned that if I keep talking, he might shit himself. You're a friendly young lady, get in there and good cop him. I'll be listening."

She took a few hesitant steps over the threshold, while Hobson moved off to look around. Now she was properly inside, she realised the size of this house. So many huge rooms, all in such a plain shade of white, so empty and without character.

The hallway leapt away above her – there was only one floor above the ground, but apparently it was important to show the volume off as much as possible, putting in this ridiculous high ceiling that could easily have contained another room. A staircase curved up around the middle.

"Hi," she said to the man cowering on the stairs, tiny in this huge vacuum. He even seemed scared of her. "So, um, do you know what happened to Jo Carlton?"

"No! I didn't do anything, I just told them about her!"

"Told who? Rush Recruitment?"

"Yes! She found out the shelf-stackers at the supermarket weren't paid, I think one of them told her, and then she complained to me."

"And you told them, and then she disappeared?"

"Yes!"

A snap went off in Angelina's head, as she realised exactly what this was. Rush Recruitment provided the workers for a low wage, and then took the money for themselves anyway. Modern-day slavery. She felt a little ill. Her teeth gritted hard for a few seconds.

"So," she said, trying to focus, "how did you get involved with them?"

"They... Anderson's Online division. I was talking to their manager and he said he'd cut warehouse costs way down thanks to Rush. I said we were having problems too and he said maybe we should look into..."

He was cut off, not by Angelina this time. Hobson yelled through from the kitchen: *"Oh for fuck's sake, not the fucking internet again!"*

Angelina didn't even smile. There was a nausea rising.

"Please, look, I'm just an accountant, I barely even wanted to be manager, I just... please..."

He was lifting himself off the stairs, motivated into fearful begging by the tone of Hobson's shout. The huge sweaty head floated into Angelina's personal space. His breath smelt.

Without thinking, she flicked her hand back and smacked Gregory James in the face, sending him crashing back down onto his arse with a wail.

Hobson arrived back in the hallway just in time to see it.

"Choi," he said, smiling for the first time in hours, "stop abusing the witness. He'll get his soon enough. We're done here."

FIVE
CONSUMER CONFIDENCE

They crashed back into the office, Choi went for the same desk she used before. Rather than flee straight into his side room, Hobson stuck around.

Stood there, playing with the lapels of his jacket. They'd barely spoken most of the way here, nothing changed now.

Choi sat down, turned on her computer, pulled off a cardigan. Stared at her still-starting monitor for a moment, then looked up at him, still not saying anything.

Finally, he went in. "Right, Choi, I've some idea of what happened here, but before we can go hardcore, I need to prove it somehow."

"Okay," she leaned forward, silence still *humming* behind her words, "what happened?"

"Basically, from what I remember of Rush, they're a big fan of using clients to do their dirty work. Avoids getting their own premises searched. So, since Anderson's Online are also a client and have connections, I reckon they were involved in taking or keeping Jo Carlton."

"Why?" She swallowed, not making eye contact. "Why would they help? If they're the ones paying Rush, why would they agree?"

"Choi, these people save you two thirds of your wage bill, sometimes more. You can't be fuckin' surprised to discover there's some shitty clauses in their client contracts."

"And if people won't obey the contract, that's when they send people like you round?"

"I suppose, well, you know, I didn't specifically do that. I was more looking after the actual employees than the clients, but…"

Hobson sighed and fixed his eyes out of the huge windows. The post-rain sun started blasting across the rooftops – not hot yet, but growing brighter. Soon he wouldn't be able to look straight at it.

"Okay, look into it, yeah? See if you can find anything on your precious internet that connects Anderson's Online to that shop at that time? I'll call around some people who might've been in the area, see if anyone saw much."

"Alright," Choi nodded, displaying no enthusiasm. "I'll try."

"Good, thanks."

She turned to her computer, just about alive and moving, began flicking the mouse about. Hobson retreated to his own office, shutting the door with a sigh. It felt like slipping into a warm bath, to be honest. Maybe he could get comfortable here.

Seconds later, he remembered it was dark, stuffy and full of files detailing his failings.

"Hobson! *Hobson!*"

"Yeah?"

"I got it! I think I found something!"

"Linking Anderson's Online to the kidnapping?"

"Yeah!"

"Okay. And what is it?"

"Well, you know what one of the main uses of Twitter is?"

"Posting pictures of either your dinner or your cock?"

"Other than those?"

"Trying to persuade people to top themselves?"

"Okay, no. It's consumer complaining. Sending angry messages to your mobile phone company because you're getting bad signal or something."

"Right. Okay."

"So I was looking through all the complaints sent to the official Anderson's Online account, and I think I found a couple of helpful ones."

"Interesting. Such as?"

"*'Still waiting for my shopping from @AndersonsOnline. Just saw one of their vans drive straight past.'*"

"Right?"

"Don't worry, it gets better. Here's the next one, twenty minutes later: *'Still no text from @AndersonsOnline, but their damn van just sped straight back the other way. Beginning to feel like they don't like me.'*"

"And where does this moaning prick live?"

"Funny you should ask. Last tweet of interest: *'@AndersonsOnline Seriously guys, the Hackney store is round the corner from me, I could've gone there and back by now. Where's my stuff?'*"

"Interesting. Very fucking interesting. I think that'll do us for confirmation. Good work, Choi."

"Thanks."

"Although while you've got it open: does he say anything else?"

"Nothing that helps us."

"Yeah, but I'm curious now. Did the bloke get his shopping?"

"Um, a few more tweets where his friends console him about the late delivery. Then eventually this: *'Shopping got here eventually, but lettuce slightly wilted. Can't recommend @AndersonsOnline to my followers, I'm afraid.'*"

"Christ. Okay, Choi, go on Twitter and call him a cunt."

"From the official company account? Because that might look bad."

"No idea what that means, but fine. Use your own, then."

"I'd rather not, sorry."

"Fuck's sake."

"Want me to start an account for you to do it?"

"No, we should probably go and rescue this kidnap victim. I'll do it when we get back."

"Okay."

Hobson turned away from the computer, face cracked wide in triumph. "Okay, Choi," he gestured towards the lift, "no time, let's move. Gotta get a call in to the Rush Recruitment shitboard before the day ends."

Choi stood from her chair, scrambling to shut down her computer and pull her coat on, check her wallet was back in her bag. Hobson was already most of the way to the lift.

"Yeah, but," she called out as her monitor clicked off, "why do we need to go somewhere to call them?"

"Once we've done the call, you need to go right into the police. I keep 'em distracted, then we tell the cops where she is so they can swoop in and save her. It'll be amazing. Ellie will love how much I'm co-operating."

"So this is all to impress the detective-sergeant ex-wife?"

Choi arrived at the exit as Hobson let the door drop shut on her face. She pushed through with a grunt to join him by the lift. And then her critique continued: "But shouldn't we see what they say before calling the cops?"

"It's about winning, Choi. If we don't call anyone and the meeting goes badly, we might not be able to stop them killing her. So we give Ellie her chance to shine."

The silence seemed longer than was natural.

"Okay," Choi eventually nodded, once the lift doors began to open. She was even smiling. "Of course."

Hobson didn't know what she was insinuating, but moved the conversation on to the weather anyway.

SIX
LAST CONTACT

In the Subway across from the police station, Hobson gazed at his sandwich, eyes tiny and far away. His craggy face seemed even more sunken and sad than before, the grey streaks in his hair standing out.

Not that Angelina was eating her lunch. In fact, she'd consumed less than her boss. Sipped her drink, checked her phone.

Hobson squinted at the staff behind the counter, dutifully stacking up those tiny cardboard trays of chicken. Eventually, he returned his eyes to Angelina and told her what was on his mind. She wished he hadn't bothered.

"Sometimes the old shit comes close to ruining places like this for me, y'know?"

"Why?"

"Because a lot of them are staffed by Rush people. Sometimes I think I can tell." He pressed the heels of his hands into the grooves of his skull. "Something dead in the eyes."

"Right."

"Mm. Fuckers, ruining my life and my sandwiches."

"Yeah."

At last, they both took another bite into their lunch, as if continuing to eat was an act of defiance against the looming threat. Hobson was so opposed to the scumbags, he kept going until hi entire foot-long sub was gone. Then he screwed up the wrapping and pulled out his crappy mobile.

"Okay, it's the end of the afternoon, we'd better get this going. Stay quiet," he said, voice soft, looking at the phone rather than her.

Angelina nodded.

Here it was again: "Hi, this is Rush Recruitment, for when you need staff NOW! No-one's in to take your call at the moment, but leave a message after the beep and we'll get back to you ASAP!"

Every time Hobson heard that fucking answerphone message, it sounded more insulting, specific, designed to take a spear to him.

He looked over at Choi. She was watching him with wary distance. Like she expected him to go apeshit any moment.

The answerphone beep ended and he directed his eyes back down at the table, pinching the bridge of his nose to block Choi from sight.

"Rush, it's John Hobson again. I've had a chat with Gregory James and the trembling bumtick gave you up in seconds. I want Jo Carlton alive or I'm taking him down to the cops and backing his dribbling up with everything I know about you. Don't take too long to fuckin' think about it."

RUSH JOBS

Hobson stumbled to a pause, as if something knocked him over the head. The full magnitude of his threat washed through him. The shock was so intense, it took concentration to terminate the call.

Even when the phone was down, he struggled to stop the handset quivering.

"You okay?" Choi said, not unkindly.

"I'll be fine. If the scum are as efficient as I remember, they should phone back in a couple of..."

And the phone rang. He picked up, ready for the most cheerful, grating voice possible.

"Hi there Mister Hobson, this is Rush Recruitment! Good to hear from you just now, would you like to make an appointment for a quick chat?"

Hobson couldn't stop grimacing. Choi chuckled as he jerked his head away from the source of pain. The operator's voice was female, perky and unbearable. He tried to work with it nonetheless. "Yeah, um, this evening please."

"That's totally fine, sir! Would you like to come on up to our offices?"

"No, I'd rather die. The Left Hand at eight, and bring Jo Carlton if you know what's good for you. My partner will turn everything over to the cops if anything happens to me."

"I'm afraid we won't be able to arrange that, but someone will be along for a talk. Hopefully we'll be able to sort an exchange out for a later date."

Hobson almost argued, but there was no point. "Yup, whatever. See you later."

"Thanks for calling, Mister Hobs..."

He hung up.

"So," Choi said, "did it happen like you expected?"

"More or less exactly. Now, I need you to do your bit."

"What if Ellie says no?"

Hobson smiled. "She won't. She never does."

"Hobson," Choi gulped, "I know having a police detective ex-wife lets you get away with a lot, but should we rely on her for everything? I mean, she seemed pretty angry last week. I don't think this is impressing her."

"Look, you don't know her. It'll be fine. Now, finish your sandwich while I head back to the tube. I'll text you when it's safe to get started."

"Okay then. See you later."

"Hope so." He got up, but struggled to storm out and get moving. Not certain why either – maybe he was getting sentimental. Or worried the threat wouldn't work and Rush would stab him.

Either way, he'd find out soon enough.

"Take care, Choi. And keep me updated."

They exchanged one last look, then he pulled his coat off the chair and headed for the door as brusquely as possible. He surveyed the staff one last time as he walked out, searching their eyes, but just couldn't see the silent, enslaved scream.

Perhaps he'd lost the knack for spotting it. Or the police station across the road made this an unsafe location for Rush people. Could be either.

About half an hour later, Angelina's sandwich was long finished and Twitter starting to bore her. Just in time, a text from Hobson came through ordering her to enter the police station across the road as planned.

Of course, she'd never been in one of those. As they'd rattled through London on the tube earlier,

Hobson told her what to do: walk up to the desk, ignore all the stares and ask for the person you want. Try not to look nervous but, y'know, don't worry — seeming suspicious might encourage them to talk to you.

She pushed through the glass doors, tuned out the grisly crime posters plastered around, focused on the desk in front of her. Thankfully, not many other people in there.

She went straight for the policeman behind the desk. He tapped at his computer, only looking up when she approached him. Immediately, a patronising smirk ripped across his face. Did she really look like a delicate middle class flower who would never enter a police station?

With a small wave, she said: "Hi, can I talk to Detective Sergeant Ellie Simons please? Tell her it's Angelina Choi and John Hobson sent me."

SEVEN
RUSH JOB

The only way to enter a dodgy bar: don't draw attention to yourself until you have to. Hobson would do the same when entering any cheap-arse McHellerman's chain pub, just to avoid attracting drunk and annoying patrons. Still, The Left Hand was a special case.

After all, it was a well-known meeting point of the North-East London underground. It served as a market for dirty goods, not to mention a venue for any off-the-books show you might want to put on. Yet, at the same time, it was a 'Heller's pub, a mass-produced same-as-the-others experience, allowing a wide cross-section of the London class spectrum to blend in.

Unlike his first visit during the horrible breakfast session, this was prime early evening boozing time. The cheap tables glistened with barely-cleaned stickiness, but no-one thought twice before claiming them. Lights glared at a constant mood-free mid-level, but at least the beer was cheap. The bulk of the pub stretched out in a long line, bar in the middle, opening up into a barely-used dinner area at the back.

That shadowed rear end was where the scary people met, and Hobson wasn't going near it this time.

Only a few sodden regulars checked him out as he entered. A reliable line of people rustled around the bar, but no awful crowds, as it was only Tuesday. Busy but not heaving. Perfect.

Hobson made straight for the drinks, hanging back in the queue to check out everyone around him. As he wedged into the rear of the small cluster, Hobson spotted a crying man in a dark corner being threatened with a knife. Elsewhere, a withered old guy with a three-pronged fork instead of a hand was talking to a woman in a huge fur coat. Hobson hoped he wasn't planning on pleasuring her with that claw.

He didn't recognise anyone though, which brought up his next big question – would he be meeting someone he knew?

Right then, the old days sauntered up to him, wearing a cheap suit and chunky watch, coloured in with fake tan.

"Alright, Hobson?" said the orange man, his rock solid spiked hair glistening awfully. "How's shit hanging?"

"Rocky." Hobson managed a handshake, but couldn't stretch to a smile. "Good to see you again."

It wasn't. Gigantic wanker.

For a moment after Angelina told Ellie about Hobson's plan, the policewoman stared darkly at her tidy desk, eyes wide and staring behind razor-straight hair. She always looked so worn out, even though she was well-dressed, professional and functional.

Her expression barely changed in all the time it took her to take in the information, make some phone calls and set off. Now Angelina sat in the passenger seat of an unmarked car, Ellie driving and a van full of policemen following along behind. She certainly kept her interior clean, Angelina noted – no stains or marks, not even any stray personal items.

A single blue light flickered above her head, other motorists diving out of their way as they tore through the early evening traffic. A small part of Angelina couldn't help but think *'Wow!'*, just on principle. She was part of a real operational police convoy, streaking off to the Anderson's Online warehouse. Behind them, a squad of well-equipped guys just raring to back them up.

"So, he's sure about this?" Ellie said, staring ahead at the dark road.

"Yeah. Um. Pretty sure. He says it's just the sort of shit Rush pull. Um. Thing they do."

"Yes, well," Ellie blinked a couple of times, accent cracking and mouth twitching downward, "he would know."

"Yeah. Plus, like I said, we found that guy on Twitter who saw their van in the area."

"True."

The conversation didn't go beyond that.

They pulled up at Anderson's Online, the others right behind them. It was a warehouse on an industrial estate full of blank buildings, the perfect place to hide something. Everything was a trade vehicle or a manager's car, no-one came here unless they had to. A world of potential secrets.

There was a huge loading bay outside, warehouse stretching away behind. As the day turned into evening, they kept working, rolling cages in and out of vehicles. One such lorry was on the way out of the gates, until the cadre of police officers pulled into the exit, stopping anyone leaving. Ellie and Angelina did the same to the staff car park.

Crashing, scowling figures began spilling out of the police van, far more than she'd expected.

Still not acknowledging Angelina more than she had to, Ellie got out of the car and leapt across the thin divide between the two car parks. Shoving through some foliage, she waved to get everyone's attention.

"Alright, guys," she yelled at her people, "the vehicles first, then the warehouse. Don't let anyone leave."

A line of men in black advanced on the building, wielding batons, screaming at anyone who made a move. Angelina felt bad right then – after all, if these were Rush employees, they were basically slaves. So nice of her to bring the police along to roar and brutalise them.

"Got promoted innit, I'm a senior account executive now," Rocky said, adjusting his cuffs. "A lot more responsibility, a lot more work hard play hard, y'know how it is."

Hobson's first thought was: *'Yeah, more like senior a-cunt executive.'* His second: *'And yet you haven't even bought my fucking pint.'*

Instead, he said: "I bet."

"So, yah, Hobson, hear you're a celebrity private dick now," he continued, gliding through syllables like a lobotomised chimp. "How's that going? Get invited to any good parties?"

"You know me, Rocky. I live for the movie premieres."

"Oh really? Any flicks I might've picked up a tickle of? Got my ear pretty down on the cultural ground, innit."

Hobson tapped the table like a drum kit. No violence, he could do this, even when he *knew* the victim deserved it. He wasn't going to let these people beat him into beating them.

He was saved from explaining the concept of *jokes* to Rocky by a certain expanse of lard and white apron undulating past their table. Chef and general pub-leader Micro was on the move as ever, carrying meals to their destinations, keeping a smile on his wide face for the various shades of bastard he serviced. That yellow stain on his left breast was particularly noxious.

"Mister Hobson," the big guy smiled. "How generous of you to grace our establishment again."

"Just having a drink with my friend here," Hobson said, the word *friend* making his stomach turn. "No trouble, Micro."

"Actually, I needed to talk to you about..."

"Not now," Hobson snapped, giving him the death stare. "Some other time. I'm sure I'll be back, I can't seem to fucking escape this place."

Micro eyed him up for a few seconds as if ready to blurt out whatever it was anyway, before remembering the two plates of food balanced on each arm. He couldn't serve them *stone* cold, that'd be a step too far.

With one last guttural noise, he sailed away. Gotta be impressed with his skill in weaving that bulk through so many close-packed flimsy tables without spilling the food.

Taking advantage of the interruption, Hobson bit into the meat of the meeting: "Okay Rocky, let's talk Carlton. Ready to hand her back in exchange for me not fucking outing you?"

"Well, that's question of the hour innit?" Rocky said, the sound of his voice making Hobson grit his teeth. "The *other* Miss Carlton on TV – phwoar, fitty – seemed determined to get her story out there. Worried us, that did."

"So if I persuade both Carltons to shut up about your business, you'll release her unharmed?"

"Yeah, killing her would be extreme shizzle, we were gonna stop at hot torture action anyway. So we're prepared to let her out as long as you take full responsibility for their silence."

Hobson pretended the word *shizzle* hadn't happened. "Meaning what?"

"Meaning if she breathes a word, we send people after you, Jo Carlton, her sister, your bitch ex-wife, that cute little Jap girl we keep seeing in the papers with you, anyone else we feel like. Dig?"

"Dig? Huh." Hobson stared down at his hands for a few moments, feeling a pounding throb grow in his temples.

Inside the warehouse, past the loading bays, Angelina stepped into the main unit and her mouth fell open. The crates of shampoo, packs of nappies, bags of crisps, gardening gear, bottled drinks, stacked and racked from here to eternity. It was like a dozen supermarkets pulled up and thrown into frames. Rollcages scattered everywhere, abandoned by workers when the police stormed in.

One middle-aged woman wore a faded grey t-shirt and jeans, similar to Angelina's look the previous day. She stared with a motionless eye as her head was held against the white wall. Thirteen policemen shut down the online supermarket operation inside ten minutes.

As products towered above her, she wandered into a large gap between all the units. Looked like the only open space in the entire warehouse area. The manager, bald and nervy in a navy suit, emerged from his office, hands above his head even though no-one was pointing a gun at him.

Ellie waited in the centre, Angelina behind her. The rest of the workforce was all under strict control, even though none looked like putting up a fight. They might try and move evidence, Angelina thought, but wasn't convincing herself.

"What's up, detective?" said the manager, his words more confident than his tone.

"Good evening," Ellie smiled. Shoving her hands deep into her coat pockets, she advanced on to the man. He had no choice but to back up until he hit a heavily padded cop. "We're looking for Jo Carlton, the woman who went missing a few days back. We had a tip saying she might be here. Would you know anything about that?"

"Not a thing, ma'am." Voice still shuddering.

"Fine. Search the place, everyone."

She gave him another stare, as the police tore up and down the aisles. Every time they smashed a box to the ground, Angelina flinched. She saw one of the workers, a skinny guy with sunken eyes, getting yelled at by a policeman at close quarters. Yes, Angelina could've asked Ellie to make him stop, but she chickened out.

Speaking of the former Mrs Hobson, she came over right then. Leaned down close and whispered in Angelina's ear: "He'd better be right about this, kid."

"Yeah," she replied, not sure what else to say. Ellie's hair was *viciously* straight.

Angelina's phone rang, her ringtone an embarrassingly twee twinkle against all this stark law enforcement. To her relief, it was Hobson. She scrambled to answer, aware Ellie was in hearing range.

"Hobson, hi, um, how's it going?"

"Badly. You found her yet?"

Angelina looked about the room again, wincing at yet another crash as they pulled a huge pile of speakers apart. "Don't think so, sorry."

"Good. Any chance you could get them to give up and leave before they do?"

"What?" mumbled Angelina.

"Long story," Hobson sighed, "but we got new problems. Sending you to the cops without speaking to Rush first may have been a bit impatient."

"Oh, well," she hissed, "shame no-one suggested that before, isn't it?"

Before he could snap back, there was a flurry of shouting from the corner by the Hi-Fi equipment. The police rolled and crunched the heavy speaker boxes away, then started tugging at the floor. Was that a trapdoor?

"Um, Hobson, I think they might be close."

"Fuckity fuck. Alright," he said, "put Ellie on."

As she handed over the phone, Angelina saw one of the police shine their torch into the darkness below the floor. A victorious yell echoed around the room.

Hobson hurried outside the pub and stood against the front wall. Kept a clear few feet of brickwork between himself and the smokers, though only after begging a cigarette and a light off them on the way past.

Tried his best to keep the agitation out of his voice when Ellie came on the line.

"Ellie, hi, listen, have you got Jo Carlton?"

"I think so, John."

"Shit, okay," Hobson said, voice speeding up, hand knocking against the wall. "You can't let her tell anyone else about Rush, okay? Get her to say it was only the online manager or maybe the kids with the hammer or something, just don't let her…"

"*John,*" she cut him off with a furious mutter. "Do you mind if I check she hasn't been starved or abused before I ask her to keep your bullshit secret?"

"Yeah, yeah, alright." Hobson spun his hand in a bored circle, almost putting out his cigarette. "Just make sure she doesn't say anything."

The phone went silent for a few seconds. If not for the fast tapping sound of steps, Hobson would've checked if the call was dead.

And then she came back. Obviously walked away from everyone else so she could yell at him.

"*Yeah, yeah, alright?* What the fuck is wrong with you? I've been keeping these Rush arseholes secret for years to stop you going to prison, which could utterly ruin me by the way. Now, let's drag someone else into it, doesn't matter if she's lost a finger or been raped and *yeah, yeah, alright?* For fuck's sake."

"Ellie, I didn't mean I don't care about…"

"No, you really don't. Fuck off, John. I hope you and your new teenage sidekick have a happy self-absorbed life together."

The phone was definitely dead this time. Hobson hadn't inhaled for a few seconds, so taking another drag to keep his hands busy only provoked a coughing fit. Ellie would be fine, he told himself. Not the first time she'd sworn at him.

Gingerly, nervous and scared next to all these burly, loud guys in heavy gear, Angelina approached the scattered and dented boxes of audio-visual kit. Once she'd made her way around all those obstacles, she saw it.

The trapdoor was a flat panel, the same blank grey colour as the rest of the hard flooring. Underneath was a small, dark space, full of dust and plastic-covered crates. A torch beam flashed across, revealing a paper plate, the packaging of an Anderson's Budget Plus sausage roll or six, all surrounded by a nest of filthy blankets.

Jo Carlton herself had already been hauled out. She sat on the warehouse floor not far away, eyes darting, nodding her head as dirt drifted out of her dulled shoulder length hair. She looked a bit like her sister, Angelina thought, but her face was smaller, features tighter.

Her suit was untorn. She still had a friendly supermarket manager's uniform, style and face, but the dust and murk made her look like a museum piece. She was her own photo from the news, zombified into life.

Angelina took a few steps in her direction, and Jo's eyes snapped across. They lit up, perhaps because she was dressed normally, rather than in Anderson's uniform or cop armour.

"Hello," Jo waved as if helping a customer. The big, irritable policeman trying to ask about her capture seemed slightly put out, but let her speak.

"Hi," Angelina said, standing over her. "I'm Angelina. Are you okay?"

The words tumbling from Jo's mouth sped up as they continued. "Just hurts, I think. They kept throwing down sausage rolls and food, but they wouldn't tell me what was happening, y'know? The cages kept rumbling over my head. It was like being at work, only it was swallowing me."

"Yeah." Angelina gulped. "And you're okay?"

She shrugged. "Had a few blankets. They didn't hurt me or anything."

"Good."

At last, Detective Sergeant Ellie arrived to take control. "Miss Carlton, I'm DS Simons. Can you give me a few minutes with her, constable?"

The policeman obeyed without question. Angelina expected to be the next one sent away, but it never happened. In fact, Ellie never acknowledged the lingering teenager at all, just knelt down next to Jo.

"Are you okay, Miss Carlton?"

She nodded again, even slower. "I think so. I was just saying to, um, her," she indicated Angelina, "nothing really happened. They just kept me."

"Okay, that's good, thank you. And do you know *why* they kept you?"

Jo stared for a few moments. "Because I found out Greg was using Rush Recruitment to get these... these slave workers into the store."

"Okay. That's what we thought. Listen, Miss Carlton, Rush are very dangerous. If you testify against them, it'll involve witness protection, changing your identity, all that, and it still might not work."

The blood drained from Jo's face, and she'd looked pale to begin with.

"If you want, we can go after the Online manager over there, maybe Gregory James too, for using unpaid labour, and they probably won't turn over Rush either. Would that be okay?"

It didn't take Jo long to agree to that, nodding fervently. Ellie finally showed Angelina her reddened eyes, and then smiled at Jo, holding out a hand to help her stand up.

"Good. Now, let's get you some proper food."

Angelina stared after Ellie and Jo as they walked away. She almost didn't bother texting Hobson to tell him he was off the hook.

Hobson got the text just in time to stub out his cigarette and toss it into the bin. On his way back into The Left Hand, he stopped to thank the guy who donated it. A smile stayed in place as he swept past the bar, back to where Rocky sat.

"Ah, Hobson, all good in our hoodarama?"

"No idea what the fuck that means," Hobson said as he slid back into the booth, "but yeah, all quiet. You might lose the Anderson's contract, but I assumed you'd be out of there soon anyway."

"True that," Rocky nodded, "we were gonna ditch them anyway to be on the side that is safe."

"Good." Hobson reached for the remains of his drink. "So we're done?"

"Yes, but remember, only as long as the girl stays quiet."

"It'll be fine, Rocko." Hobson smiled, calm at last. "I got contacts. But there is one more loose end you might need to deal with."

"Really? Well, Hobs-man, my ears are open and ready to receive."

'Don't punch him,' Hobson's mind whispered over and over. *'You still can't punch him.'*

Soon enough, everything folded away back into that police van. They took Jo Carlton, as well as the increasingly uncool manager of Anderson's Online. Also apprehended: one of the workers who was stupid enough to fight back against the search.

He was a small guy in ripped jeans who took a swing at a policeman's heavy padding with a box of waterbottles. The cop staggered forward, but by the time he'd worked out who to blame, his equally protected mates took care of business for him.

They didn't beat the perp up. Instead, one arm twisted behind his back harder than necessary, they tossed him into a van.

Angelina looked around for Ellie and she was watching, teeth gritted.

"C'mon, kid," she said, pointing towards her car, "can I drop you off at the station?"

"I…" It was fast becoming the evening, and that was rather out of her way. "Any chance of somewhere more south maybe please?"

"I can leave you near Old Street for the tube. Other than that, not really."

"Okay." Ellie didn't seem open to negotiation, have to make do. "That'd be great, thanks."

EIGHT
SAD RECEPTIONIST

Angelina could've gone back home or to the office. The tube lines stretched out before her, real tunnels representing her imagined choices. Her family would eventually see on the news how famous detective John Hobson recovered a kidnap victim. Obviously, then they'd text to accuse her of reckless self-endangerment.

This would have been an ideal moment to sit in the pub alone. But she was sixteen, two years under the legal drinking age. Worse, she looked about fourteen and didn't have an adult to buy drinks for her.

Not to mention, hunching over in bars looked boring. If she wanted to stare soulfully into space, Angelina would damn well do it in her bedroom where she could put loud music on and cry if she wanted.

Instead, she found her way to Peckham's Brightman Business Centre. This would be it, she told herself. After a day of watching the adults disappoint her, she would get something done. She'd finally ask Will out, or at least have a conversation with him. Maybe wave, say '*Hi!*', pretend she was fetching something from the old office.

Just like in the first week, she skipped around a few tiny corner shops, their rubbish from the day in piles outside. Every night in South London, the streets looked like a long, straight dump.

Angelina scampered up to the door of the Brightman, then swore as she realised she no longer had a key card. Even worse, Will wasn't at his desk either. The shutter hadn't dropped, the centre was open until seven, he shouldn't have gone home yet. Must've decided it was late enough to get away with running to the toilet and leaving the desk vacant.

She knocked on the glass door, but no response. Tried again, feeling her heart rate spiking. The longer she smacked the window like a sad orphan, the less casual, cool and spontaneous her cover story of '*just passing by*' would sound.

People on the pavement gave her pitying glances. Angelina turned back to the glass and punched it so hard, her hand sparked out in pain. Should've gone home and put that loud music on.

Even worse, her eyes were dampening right there in the street. Before she could find a quiet café to give up in, there was a flash of bright red in the corner of her vision. It went from the floor up to above her head, interrupted only by a silky shirt and dark-skinned face, before resuming as a garish top hat. The Pimp.

"Hey hey," he said, in his deep accent. Angelina felt her feet shaking. "What's up with you, little girl?"

"I… um. Just. I. Um." Angelina said, badly.

"I getcha. I'm picking up what you're putting down here. You're Johnny's girl, right?"

Angelina wanted to scream. Instead, she took a moment. She could never exist in Hobson's world if she spontaneously combusted because a tall black guy in a silly costume spoke to her.

So she spoke, keeping her voice level. "I suppose. But please don't call me that, it's weird."

"Fair play, missy. Are you waiting for Big Willy?"

Missy? "Well, I'm just popping in to pick up some stuff from the old place."

"So you're still working with Johnny?"

"Yeah."

"Cool. Can you get him to call me on 'morrow? Me and Benny, we got troubs, and he ain't answering his mobile."

"Troubs? Who's Benny?"

"Big troubs. Don't worry."

Angelina nodded. "Sure. Why not?"

"Sweet. Thanks, missy. See you soon."

He raised a hand, she flinched automatically, but realised he was holding it up to her for a quick shake. She accepted, smiled, nodded and let him go.

At last, there was a knock on the glass behind her. She turned around and there was Will, hair carefully floating across his face as ever, raising an eyebrow at her. He punched the door release button and swung it open.

"Hi, Lina," he said, with a polite smile.

"Will, hey." Don't blush, for the love of God.

"Sorry, you weren't out here long were you?"

"No, I was fine." She glanced up and down the street, checking The Pimp wasn't nearby to disagree with her.

"Cool." He let the door drift free and made back for his desk, still crammed in at one side. He was wearing a pair of brownish skinny trousers and a loose shirt over a tight t-shirt. Angelina forced her eyes upwards when he turned round.

"Hi," she said again. "I just wanted to check the old office, I think we left something. Could you maybe let me have a key?"

"Not really, I'm afraid. New company moved in this morning."

"Already?" She laughed. "That quickly? Here?"

"Hey," Will laughed, "don't diss the 'ham. This place is on the up and up, we got cool rooftop bars and, well, obviously some hipsters." He gestured down at himself with a playful smile. "I think it's a marketing company."

"They're not called Social Awesome are they?"

"Say what?"

"Never mind." She made herself smile. "So how are you?"

"Not much has changed since you saw me yesterday, Angelina. Squeezing into my desk, signing in guests, chasing away tramps. You?"

"Oh, we solved a kidnapping. I found out some stuff about Hobson, it was…" She checked herself. "Weird. It was weird."

"Wow. Your life sounds pretty exciting to my sad receptionist's ears. Maybe I should open a detective agency."

"Oh, you *should*," she said, voice jumping up. "It'd be fun. I'll come work for you!"

"Ah," he laughed as her feet danced on the ground. "But I'd have to close my comedy Twitter account *@SadReceptionist*, my followers would be devastated."

She giggled, and he reached behind his desk. "Anyway, before I forget, since you mentioned *stuff*, we found this in Hobson's old office. Is it yours?"

He rustled underneath for a second, plastic thudding sound emerging as he pulled out a drawer. When his hand emerged, it held a thin purple scarf, different shades of yarn running across the length. She'd been wearing it on the first day. Not even realised it was gone.

"Thanks!" she rushed over to grasp it, failing to brush her hand against his.

"Yeah, I didn't think it was really Hobson's colour."

This time, Angelina held back the full-on titter, not wanting to sound hysterical. Looked at the scarf for a few seconds, before wrapping it back round her neck.

"Thanks, Will."

"Any time. So, I guess you're definitely leaving forever, now that you're a cool East London girl. Plus your work experience ends soon, doesn't it? Is it still two weeks?"

"Um, I'm not sure. Hobson's not really said much about it, and it's been kinda weird. Not as good as last week."

"Yeah? I thought you were loving it."

"Why'd you think that?" Angelina felt her eye narrowing.

"Dunno. Just something in the way you walked."

Her throat emitted a gasping gulp sound at that, she sputtered out a cough to cover.

"I don't know," she said slowly, winding herself up in her mind. Now or never. "Anyway, even if Hobson fires me, I could always come back down here. Did you want to meet up some time, maybe?"

A pause stretched out for a while, or perhaps it was all in her head. She tried to at least keep eye contact. Mustn't back out of the door before he could reply.

"Sure," he said, "why not? Add me on Facebook, I'm William Herrison."

Trying not to split her own face with the grin, she nodded, smiled and shouted a vague goodbye. Even managed to operate the door without smacking into the glass. Strolled away down the road walking on air, danced around piles of trash and made it back to the station.

Only then did she pull out her phone to see a text from her Mum: *'Just saw you and your detective helped rescue that woman – well done!!! Xx'*

Wow. Despite the day she'd had, this was the best ten minutes ever. She pulled up her Twitter app, followed the *@SadReceptionist* account, started reading some of the tweets.

They were actually funny, thank God.

NINE
THE HAMMER FALLS

Considering he was a grown fucking man, it took Hobson a shameful amount of time to pick up the phone and make that call. But at last, he settled on his intro: "Michelle, it's John Hobson, how's it going?"

"Oh, Mister Hobson, hi, did you hear the police found Jo?"

"Well, I did most of the legwork, but yeah, I suppose they did."

"They mentioned you, don't worry."

"Very big of them."

"But thank you so much Mister Hobson, we all really appreciate it."

"Call me John, it's fine. So, Michelle, I was just wonderin'..."

"Oh, yes, the money, of course. Don't worry, Mister H... John, I won't make this awkward, you've earnt it. How much do we owe you?"

"Well, that wasn't what I..." Hobson moved the phone away from his head for a second. "Yeah, it was only a couple of days, so let's say a grand?"

"Is that all?"

"It's all good, Michelle. They rent me this office pretty cheap, thanks to my old mate Pete The Wolf Lunatic."

"Oh. Well, that's nice. Can I just take your bank details, John? Or do you need to send me an invoice?"

He agreed on an address for said invoice – must show Choi how to do those for him – and the call sank to a conclusion not long after. Maybe some other time, he told himself. Asking Michelle out just after he superheroed her sister would be taking advantage anyway.

Hobson put the phone down and walked out of his boxy personal office. Hovered in the bigger space outside where Social Awesome once lived. There were eight desks spread across the room. This should be a home for a real company where people worked, chatted, flirted, went out for lunch, all that shit. Not a quiet tomb for John Hobson to feel sorry for himself. Why the fuck was he here? Next week, he might not even have a work experience kid to fill one stupid empty space.

Maybe he should call Rocky. Get Rush to send over some unpaid slaves to put arses on seats, go through old Edward Lyne files, take his incoming calls. They'd do it too, just to spite him.

He brought a fist the size of a tankard through some shitty plastic in-tray. It splintered and cracked in half, his hand bounced off the desk underneath. He examined the skin; a few scratches but nothing too bad. Have to get rid of the wreckage before Choi came in tomorrow, assuming she turned up. Couldn't blame her if she didn't. He stared out of the window, wondering whether he'd bother replacing her.

"John."

He turned around, though he'd known who was there before moving a muscle. The streetlights rippled through the dark room.

"Ellie." Her big coat was buttoned shut, face tight and staring, eyes peering sharply between the falling tresses of hair. Even though he knew she'd been off in an evil warehouse and could see the dust and grot on her clothes, she seemed strangely immaculate. He never heard her come in either. Perhaps she was a ghost or figment of his imagination?

Trying to re-establish some control, he said: "Don't I have a receptionist to keep intruders out?"

"Tell them you're police and they tend to get out of the way."

"I've heard. So, what brings you down this way?"

Making her way over from the doorway, she stood next to him, gazing out over the shitty buildings of East London. At least the South was straight up tumbledown. Over here, he felt it was somehow an affectation. The environment was *ironically* falling apart. Or maybe Hobson was projecting his hatred of hipsters onto their brickwork.

"I've spent all day dealing with your shit, John," Ellie said. "Had to bury the security tape of that supermarket break-in, and by the way, did it not *occur to you* that they might have CCTV?"

He gave it his best grin. "I knew I could count on you, Ellie."

"Yeah. Was it you who mashed up that kid as well?"

"He nicked Choi's mobile," Hobson said. "You can't make any fucking concessions to these people."

"Yeah," she caught his eye. "Yeah, I'm beginning to see that."

"What does *that* mean?"

"It means... Look, I wanted to believe that if I made it as easy as possible for you, maybe you'd give this detective thing a proper shot. Maybe the guy I married might manage to claw his way back out."

"And now?"

"I'm just enabling you. Sorry, John. Call me when you're trying harder."

Her eyes glistened in the moonlight. Hobson felt something drop away under him. "Ellie, look, I didn't beat anyone up for months, I can totally..."

"Yeah, and even that didn't last."

"I called you about the kidnapping rather than trying to save the fuckin' day myself!"

"So you want a medal for bothering to let the police do their jobs?"

"I'm not doing anything wrong, I saved Jo Carlton, I caught Pete Vole, I..."

"And a load of Social Awesome people died! And Rush Recruitment got away with it again! And some kid with cracked bones is locked up for breaking into a supermarket using a hammer he can barely lift! This is just the old days all over again."

She creaked into a broken, squeaky impression of his voice. "*I know the slavery's a bit rough, Ellie, but I'm not actually locking them up, just guarding the vans!*

There's no difference, John. Not being a full twat doesn't let you off for aiding and abetting. Read the fucking law."

"Ellie, I'm sorry, I know I was harsh earlier, but I never meant to…"

"John, don't." She wiped her hand over her eyes. "Enough. And let that poor work experience girl go, for fuck's sake."

"Can't, I need her to…"

"To what? Forgive you?"

"Mostly answer the phones."

"Of course. Bye then, John." Ellie shook her head, eyes down at the floor, and gave Hobson a wave as she made for the door. It shut behind her, and the lift opened wide beyond that.

He stared after her for a moment, some kind of apology hovering in his throat. Never made it out, of course.

Good job Hobson wore heavy boots. He stomped his way to Greg James' house so hard he might've damaged his feet, pausing only to sit down on the tube. Nearly walked through a couple of people on the underground.

Rocky stood in the same bus shelter Hobson and Choi used earlier in the day, accompanied by some nameless (and presumably payless) thugs. Fuck. This wouldn't be anywhere near as enjoyable as he hoped if he spoke to that nob. Best make it quick.

The awful voice rang out as Hobson approached. "Hobsonio, glad you made it. Want to meet your replacements?"

"No, I fucking do not," Hobson said, nodding sharply at the house. "Is he in there? Are we on?"

"Oh yah yah. Just like we brainstormed earlier."

"Good. I'll be going in first, you guys try not to be arseholes, okay?"

Hobson barely gave them time to nod before veering off towards the door. Thank God there was never any traffic in the hellish suburbs. He might've needed to pause before crossing the road, giving Rocky time to utter more words.

He smashed his hand against the front door – just hitting something felt good – and it rattled in its frame. No response for a few seconds, Hobson felt a smile grow on his face at the prospect of kicking the thing through.

A couple of clicks shook out and it began to open. Damn.

But Gregory James, at least, looked terrified as ever. His body somehow raced through the years from thirties to middle-aged, tired, decrepit and beaten down. He was still wearing the same loose shirt as earlier, stains spattered all down it. Booze on his breath, face quivering as he pulled the door open and tried a smile to Hobson. Gregory James wanted them to share a knowing nod as equals, but it only hung there, embarrassing him.

"Evening, Greg." Hobson stepped through the door, forcing the homeowner towards the stairs. Slammed the front door behind him – anything to delay Rocky and chums arriving.

"What… What do you want?" he said, straining to compose himself.

"Well, you may have gathered from the news that the kidnapping is over. Jo Carlton has been recovered, the police will be over to arrest you shortly."

"I… I was… I mean, I was hoping if I just confessed everything, they might go easy on me. Do you think they'll go easy on me, Mister Hobson?"

"To be honest, that's my big concern. You might tell the cops a bit too much in your fucking desperate quest for love, and that doesn't suit me. So I've come up with an alternative."

His face went full-sheet white. "Oh God, are you going to k… k… kill me?"

"Don't be silly, Greg – I'm against violence now. So I've had a chat with Rush Recruitment and persuaded them to try something new. You said you were an accountant, so they're gonna see if they can sell your services. About time they moved on from this workhouse bullshit to incorporate office skills."

"You're going to… they're… I'm a slave?"

"Yes. I would feel bad, Greg, but you utterly deserve it. Now, I *do* apologise for this part," Hobson added, reaching for the front door latch, "but I'm about to let an utter dickhead into your house."

As Rocky and his flunkies breezed in to take Gregory James away, Hobson wondered if he should feel worse about this. But it was Greg or him, and he didn't have much respect for this guy's basic human rights. Don't hire unpaid workers if you're not willing to end up one – that should be enshrined in law somewhere.

TEN
TEXTUAL ANALYSIS

"The fucking thing is, Tony, how exactly do you spill a goose? What does that even mean? Did you blend it first?"

It was nearly nine o'clock at night in the Spilled Goose, a gastropub in Walthamstow. Hobson only arrived about twenty minutes ago, but he'd been drinking most of the way there too, using an empty water bottle while on public transport to disguise the vodka.

"Or is it a metaphor? Is it like your eggs are scrambled? Your goose is cooked? Your goose is spilled, which means what exactly? That there's still a chance to pick it back up again?"

"Dunno mate," Tony said, choking back a laugh. A wave of rage reared up at the back of Hobson's mind – was he being mocked? Not noticing, his friend continued: "I mean, this is a fairly new pub, y'know the sort of thing. Landlord probably just thought it sounded cool."

Hobson looked around the interior. The decor itself wasn't too bad – sturdy wooden furniture, low lighting, a few more wanky paintings on the wall than he'd like, but otherwise fine. He was getting on in years, couldn't drink in dive bars and McHellerman's chain shitholes forever.

Admittedly, he was by far the oldest person here. The furniture didn't creak when he leant on it, which seemed inauthentic.

"Yeah," he concluded at last. "Fuckers."

"Right. So what's up, Johnny?"

Tony's voice hit a small notch of annoyance, and Hobson forced his eyes back front and centre, rather than glancing around the place. Good quality joists in the ceiling, though.

"What?"

"What's wrong?" He rubbed his bald head, always a sign he was getting worked up. "You called half an hour ago and demanded this meet-up. I do have a life outside you, y'know. My wife wasn't thrilled."

"Oh, y'know, me and Ellie had a fight."

"Fucking hell." The head-rubbing looked like it might erode his scalp. "It's like three years ago all over again."

"Just, you know, I needed a tiny help with a case, and she had to get pissy about it."

"Johnny, I know she does you the occasional favour, but I don't think she ever agreed to be Commissioner Gordon to your Batman. You can't take it too hard if she decides to set some limits."

"Urgh." Hobson took another long swig of his beer. "It's just another kick in the nuts at the end of a shitty day."

Tony sipped his own drink. "Why? What happened?"

"Well," he leaned forward, crashing his glass down onto the chunky table with a hard thunk and splash, "you'll never guess who I ended up seeing again?"

Just as he wound up to that big reveal, Hobson's phone produced a couple of shrill text message bleeps. He reached into his pocket, fumbling for longer than was dignified, big fingers sliding over the smooth outside of his suit trousers.

Once he'd plucked the grey plastic brick out, he opened the message up with a few punts of rubber buttons. A couple needed to be pressed twice before they responded, not even counting the times he missed and hit the wrong ones.

"Oh, excellent," he said, too loud, "Tony, it's her!"

"Ellie?"

"No! Choi!"

From the self-conscious expression on Tony's face, other people must be starting to look over now. Fuck 'em.

"Right. So what does the kid want? Why is she texting you this late?"

"I'll tell you. She says," he coughed, adjusting his voice for reading aloud, *"Hey, Hobson, just letting you know I ran into the Pimp in Peckham and he said they've got big troubs, whatever that means, and could you call him? I said I'd pass it on, but didn't commit to anything. See you tomorrow.*"

Hobson scratched his head and read it again in silence, while Tony checked his own mobile and tapped out some mysterious note.

"So, Tony, what do you reckon she means?"

"Pretty much what she said?"

"Oh yeah, I know about that, I've been ignoring the Pimp's calls for hours because I couldn't be arsed, but Choi's tone was very distant, don't you reckon? A bit disinterested in my fuckin' welfare after a very traumatic day."

"You're her boss, not her girly mate. Although if this conversation about text messages goes on much longer, I might change my mind about that."

"No, see, you don't understand, some stuff happened today and I'm a bit worried she may think I'm a cunt now."

"Okay," Tony sighed, his fingers dancing out another quick message. "Just give me a couple of seconds to apologise to my family again, then you can tell me all about it."

"So, Angelina, what are you going to do once you finish at Mister Hobson's agency?"

"Oh, you know." Angelina kept her eyes directed at the knobbly raised vine pattern on the edge of her Mum's white dinner plates. "Wait for my exam results. Read a book. Maybe get a job in a shop."

Her leg shook involuntarily on that last point. Her ready meal lasagne was reduced to a few slops smeared around the plate, while the collection of family pictures and tasteful ornaments glared down around her.

Everything was such a swirly green or blue. So much thought gone into being so forgettable. She used to feel the same about the family portraits, but recently, she'd look at the three of them sitting in some studio or near a statue or whatever, all smiling thinly, and think – *That is weird, isn't it? The two white people and their Asian kid? Were other people thinking about how weird that was?*'

Not that she ever mentioned these feelings to her parents, of course.

Her Mum sat at the other end of the clean, rectangular wooden table. Her own food went long ago, but that didn't deter her from sitting in on her daughter's meal.

She'd texted Hobson just before her Mum sat down, thinking this would be a good quiet time. Luckily, it was taking him ages to respond.

"A shop?" Her Mum raised a thoughtful eyebrow. They were thick, bushy and looked pleased to be joining the rest of her hair up top. "So you aren't going to try and stay on with Mister Hobson?"

"Why?" Angelina looked up from her dinner so quick, her neck hurt for a second. "Do you think there's a chance?"

"I don't know. Do you want to? Has he said anything?"

Her Mum was leaning into the table as she spat those last two questions, and Angelina felt like a sheep herded into a conversational paddock.

"I dunno." Angelina adjusted her sitting position. "I mean, it's a hard job sometimes, but if he wants me to, I might consider it." Her rambling voice was almost ready to spill a few of her discoveries about Hobson's past, but she pulled it back.

"Angelina, I wish you'd try and tell us why it's so important you stay with this detective. I didn't realise you even cared so much."

Her plate was empty now, so when her phone twinkled out, Angelina seized it like a rope in the open sea. "Anyway, Mum, I gotta go," she said, without looking at the screen, "important detective business."

"Okay," she nodded quietly, "just take care."

Angelina didn't even reply to that, just swung around the two flights of twisting stairs leading to her loft. She wasn't sure why her parents allowed her this personal space at the top of the house, considering she mostly used it to get away from them.

Her room was as immaculate as ever, only a few small post-it notes surrounding her expensive lumbar-supporting computer chair. The tranquil pastel purple gave the room a fresh spring feel, even at night. Beneath the glow of her artful spotlight-style lighting, she flicked her laptop open to get it started, then read Hobson's text.

'Thanks, Choi. I've given him a text, we'll see what he wants. Hopefully a nice easy job, eh?'

She sighed. Hadn't he realised from her last message that she didn't want them to have anything to do with The Pimp because he creeped her out?

"You *told her* about the Rush Recruitment stuff?"

"Maybe a little. Just a bit, y'know, in summary, Tony, a tad."

"How *much* of a fucking tad?"

"Enough to hate me, but not enough to put together a full dossier for the filth."

"Johnny, for fuck's sake."

"What? If she's going to be working with me, she deserves to know why…"

"Why does she deserve to know? Why is she working with you at all?"

"Why do you care?"

"Because it involves me! I may not have been on their pay roll, but I was about, helped keep you going, I don't wanna be asked too much shit."

"Ah, you'll be fine. Choi's a good kid. Anyway, shush, I gotta text The Pimp, since I told Choi I already had."

"Why are you getting involved? That guy's weird."

"Tony, I need a *good* case, okay? Like a *good guy* case. I'm sick of other people forcing me to look like a scumbag. So either The Pimp will ask me to do something dirty and I'll tell him to get fucked and Choi will be impressed, or it'll be something I can look good doing. It's a win-win."

"This sounds like a terrible idea."

"You're no fun today."

"Sorry, Johnny, I suppose I'm just distracted by my oncoming arrest."

"Look, Choi's bright, she knows not to do anything stupid. She wouldn't want me to get arrested."

"Didn't you *just* say she hates you?"

"Yeah, but in a teenage kinda way."

"God."

"Hey, a text from The Pimp. Let's see what he wants, eh?"

"Can't wait."

"Oh, this is excellent. I think we can definitely get on board with this. Choi is gonna love it."

Angelina was pacing around her room. Despite having a decent sized personal loft which let her get a vigorous circuit going, it still felt redundant after thirty or forty loops.

She'd texted Hobson back: *'I guess, but maybe find out what he wants before we commit? I don't want to end up handing out leaflets at his business events or something.'*

With that done at last, she slumped back on her bed, dragging her laptop off its cable to accompany her. Stared at the ceiling, admiring the way the lights circled around the joins. Didn't occupy her for long, though.

In the end, she went on Facebook and started a conversation with her friend Zoë about her latest office work experience adventures. She'd been shown ways to improve her mail merge technique today and was *beyond thrilled* about it.

Angelina leaned back in her seat. Even if she was having doubts about Hobson, always good to be reminded things could be worse. Fuck, what if she *did* end up working in a shop next week?

Hobson slammed down the final dregs of his current pint. Was that his fifth? On top of anything he'd drunk before coming here? No wonder he was struggling to spell his text messages.

As soon as the glass was down, before Hobson could utter a single syllable, Tony reached for his jacket. The pub was winding down - it was a Tuesday, after all, and only the unemployed, miserable or truly alcoholic were still out. Nearly eleven o'clock, the barmaids were starting to wipe tables. Every so often, one of them took a concerned sideways glance at that big guy who kept making needlessly expansive gestures.

She had a large blonde plait and a very flattering skirt. Definitely attractive, but Hobson was at an age where he noted the physical characteristics of younger females in a very academic way. After all, she was about twenty-two, he was rocketing towards fifty. What would be the point of overthinking it?

And was it a bit depressing that he took this attitude even when drunk?

"Okay, Johnny," Tony said, already a few steps from the table, "I'm gonna head home if that's alright."

"Yeah, sure." Hobson stood up, more unsteady than he'd like. He almost asked if he could crash out in Tony's spare room, but even now, he could tell it wouldn't go over well.

"Try not to overshare with the kid, okay? Even if you must keep her around to reassure you that you're a jolly good chap, she doesn't need to know *everything* you've ever done."

"Dammit, that's what Ellie said."

"Sorry, man. Take care, yup?"

And then he was gone.

He took another look at The Pimp's latest text. He was mostly certain this was the sort of gig Choi would approve of. Maybe eighty or ninety percent sure. So he'd better take it – after all, the next case could be even worse.

Fuck Rush Recruitment, his glorious redemption began tomorrow. He texted Choi one last time: *'No worries, I've checked, it's a good job. They want to see us tomorrow in Peckham, meet me at the station first thing?'*

ELEVEN
BIG TROUBS

Angelina leapt onto the platform at Peckham Rye station. The train door beeped to a close behind her and rattled away, metal parts smashing against each other, smell of fuel rising up from the depths. The big London terminals with their huge sheets of glass seemed less raw and *mechanical* than these out of town sheds. No wonder Peckham trains huddled in the corner of London Bridge station where no-one could see them.

She scuttled around the cream-painted, brown-stained walls of the stairwell, smells rising up. It was like the bathroom in some ratty public hall – it didn't *belong* to anyone, so if cleaning took longer than ten minutes, why bother?

Sidestepping the bigger sticky patches, she made her way down. It was after nine in the morning on Wednesday, her second week at the agency was trickling away. The thought made her walk faster, as if she could out-run the need to make a decision.

Angelina Choi was one of the few passengers escaping the platforms, while a riot surged the other way. Hobson's hulking frame became visible, looming at the back of the hall. He was almost the size of a ticket machine.

He raised a hand once he saw her, gave a nod, but the smile wasn't as bright and clear as usual.

"Alright, Choi?" he said once she drew close enough to hear, his voice rumbling over the bustle of passing cheap-suits and beards.

"Morning, Hobson." Once she'd replied, he pointed out of the door. Without any further exchange, they turned out of the station. Next was a small covered walkway, shops opening up on either side.

The flow of people dried up, and Angelina saw spots of colour in the crowd moving towards them. Neon jackets, logos on the back, converging on their central position. Angelina didn't much see them in her own out-of-centre neighbourhood, but whenever she came into town, they always swarmed: the *chuggers*.

Charity muggers, street fundraisers, call them what you like. People with clipboards who want your bank details for a good cause.

As a self-questioning, socially conscious young woman, Angelina dreaded them. She knew she wasn't doing enough (anything) for charity, and didn't want her journey from A to B disrupted by a rush of guilt.

Hobson put it more succinctly: "What a shower of cunts."

"Ah, come on," she muttered back, "they're just trying to help."

"Bullshit, Choi. If they care that much about whatever cause, volunteer for it and leave me alone."

Angelina stuck close to Hobson until they were past the looming bright yellow-green anoraks, through a claustrophobic passageway onto Peckham high street. The local shops were opening up, commuters clearing out and regulars heading out for their groceries.

Hobson looked up and down the rows of windows as if he'd forgotten something.

"Where the fuck's Benny?" he demanded.

"Who?"

"Bible-Amp Benny. The guy from outside the station, dragging the microphone and amp wailing about fire and brimstone. Black, skinny, scary but lovable."

"Oh yeah, him," Angelina said, looking over her shoulder back at the station facade. Truth be told, she usually stared at her shoes in this neighbourhood, but the description sounded familiar.

"Yeah." Hobson stopped twirling and started out towards their old office. "I didn't think he'd leave that station at commuting time unless someone killed him. Maybe they have."

"Maybe," she agreed, although in her head, she was panicking about their direction. They'd be back at the Brightman Business Centre soon enough, where Will would be settling in for a hard day on reception. She'd added him on Facebook late last night but hadn't yet opened communications. Could've found him on her phone before even going home, but mustn't seem too keen. The last thing she wanted was a casual conversation between Will and Hobson at this sensitive time.

As her pulse roared towards a heavy metal drumbeat, Hobson's eyes darted off across the road. Angelina followed suit, spotting the massive red top hat of The Pimp, bobbing up and down as he fidgeted in place. He sat at a spindly grey table outside a local café, the toe-tapping demeanour, bright-red style and heavy-set frame contrasting hard with his dejected companion.

Didn't take long to recognise the skin-and-bones body of Benny, helped by the amp-shaped battered holdall at his feet and old brown jacket over plain blue and black cotton.

"Oi," Hobson roared in greeting, and the two of them turned to wave. Hobson was so keen to get over there, he almost rushed out in traffic. Eventually, he sighed and forced himself over to the next legal crossing.

They were at the café soon enough, shaking hands with The Pimp, whereas Benny only got a nod. He scraped a few chairs over so Hobson and Angelina could join the others, even though the table wasn't big enough. She felt so happy they weren't going to see Will, she almost didn't mind sitting near The Pimp.

They ordered coffees. Hobson got as far as saying "So, guys, this is Choi, she's my new…" before The Pimp chimed in, big smile, to say: "Yeah, we've met, haven't we?" His voice was syrupy and disgusting.

Angelina felt the reply sticking in her throat, and Hobson must have noticed, since he cut the exchange off a second later: "So, guys, I read your text last night, but let's have a full briefing. Why does Benny look like he's ready to finally embrace his beloved afterlife?"

"It's the chuggers," Benny said, nodding towards the station with a groan, "the damned chuggers. They moved in and now they dominate my world like some plague. How can I put the Word before people's eyes when they won't look up?"

"It ain't right, Johnny," The Pimp chimed in. "This is *our* area, but now there are so many middle class white commuters, the clipboard-fuckers have arrived."

"I hear you, guys," Hobson said, sipping his coffee. "Thank God you sent for me."

"So you'll help us?"

"Benny, after all the office internet twattery I've dealt with lately, this is just what the doctor ordered. I won't even charge much."

Angelina gulped.

"So, Choi," Hobson turned to her, "looks like you'll get to see some real street detective work. Excited?"

"Definitely," she said, resolutely professional, "I'm sure I'll learn a lot."

Throughout this meeting, Hobson kept *looking* at her expectantly, as if she was meant to be beyond excited. Angelina wasn't sure why.

As ten o'clock arrived, the street population of Peckham moved from commuters to local residents. The white-to-black ratio tilted the other way, chatter and noise picked up.

Hobson noticed his intern shifting in her chair, but he'd worked here for years before moving out east, and already missed this buzz and mess. People going about their lives in a straightforward way relaxed him. The backdrop of self-aware hipsters had the opposite effect.

Benny sipped his last few mouthfuls of tea and reached down for his bag. "Gents, I must be leaving you. The working world awaits."

"Have a good day, Benny," Hobson nodded. "Sell them flats."

Choi surprise-squinted at the news Benny had a day job as a letting agent, Hobson almost laughed at her ridiculous askew expression. His good mood petered out when he noticed The Pimp giving her a lecherous glance. So the last time wasn't a one-off, then.

"Choi, c'mon," Hobson said, motioning into the café. "Let's pay and get going, work to do."

She was on her feet in seconds. Benny hadn't even stood up himself to leave yet.

"Guys," Hobson addressed the table, "I'll ask around and get back to you about your chugger problem. Hopefully we can reclaim the streets, yeah?"

With suitable cheer, they gave big smiles and thanked him in unison.

Hobson headed through the door into the café itself, floating with vindicated glee. Choi tripped over a binbag as she headed around the table to join him. Stumbling through the door, she barely avoided stacking it into a chair.

He grabbed her shoulder and jarred her to a halt. Choi brushed his hand off to hiss at him. "Why does everyone leave their fucking rubbish on the streets around here?"

"Swearing, Choi? That's not like you."

"Yes, well." She blushed without letting up her rage. "It's annoying."

"I hear you. And why do they have a whole bag of crap at nine in the morning, eh?"

They squeezed past four or five other tables in the small café interior. It was cramped, but he could imagine it being cosy. This was the takeaway time of day, already a queue of three or four people waiting for bacon rolls to go. Only one was wearing a suit.

The detectives joined the back of the line. Hobson could hear Choi breathing in, fidgeting, about to ask some probing teenage question. He picked the wallet out of his jacket and tried to head it off with one of his own.

"So, pretty good case, eh? Can't object to screwing over *those* people."

She grunted, not even smiling, before asking her question anyway. "So what's your plan for dealing with these chuggers? I mean... do we have one yet?"

"Not as such," he said, shrugging. "It'll come to me."

"We're not going to beat them up, are we?"

"Well, *you* certainly fucking won't."

"Hobson, please can we not? I mean... That isn't the kind of detective work I wanted to be doing, you know? I'm not even sure this case is a good idea."

He looked down at her. She had the eyes-wide pleading look he'd seen before on other people, usually at bad times.

So he gritted his teeth, bit back his disappointment and gave her a firm nod of agreement. "Yeah, okay Choi. No punching. No anal clipboard insertion. Pacifism all the way."

Like a little moralistic pixie, Choi smiled and nodded. Then she snapped out of the conversation to peer ahead and tap her foot with queue impatience.

Angelina was so relieved at extracting that promise of non-violence from Hobson, she managed to follow him out of that café, up the long main street and down a familiar side-road before self-awareness hit her again.

"Hobson," she began, "where are we going?"

"Check on the old homebase," Hobson said, "see if Will's noticed anything. Just trying to get the churn going."

"The churn?"

"Stimulate ideas out of my brain. I know you kids look shit up on the internetopedia and then charge off on whatever comes up first, but we old school professionals like to do proper research."

"I never cite Wikipedia. It's unreliable."

"Aren't you a special little flower? Here we are."

Hobson reached up to the glass door of the Brightman, ignored the intercom and whacked it. Angelina couldn't think of any way to avoid this now.

So she bolted her smile into place, before the door flew open and Will leaned out. "Guys. You two just don't want to leave, do you?"

"This isn't a nostalgia trip, Will," Hobson said, barking the words more than needed. "We're here for work. Got a second?"

"Sure thing, Hobson. C'mon in."

Will slotted himself back behind his desk, and leaned forward, calmly detached as ever. As Angelina entered behind the boss, he gave her a small smile. "Morning, Angelina."

"Hi, Will." She did her trademark flappy wave, because why not? The small, thin space shot in to enclose her, feeling almost homely. Like she was coming back from the big city to visit the small town where she grew up.

"So, what's up, Hobson?" Will said. "You don't want me to let you into the old office, do you?"

"No mate, it's about the chugger problem at the station. Some of the locals want us to get them gone."

"Is it Bible-Amp Benny?"

"Hit the nail on the head."

"Yeah," Will said, laughing. "I dunno, fundamentally I'm in favour of their causes, but I'm not a big fan of the harassment approach. Just doesn't seem alright, y'know? At least Benny stays out of my personal space."

"Exactly!" Angelina exclaimed.

As she blushed, Hobson carried on. "Right, so any idea how we get them to fuck off? I was considering trying to organise an uprising, but that…" His eyes flicked towards Angelina. "That just seems too violent, y'know?"

"You could start a petition on the internet?" Will said, eyes lighting up. "Get some grassroots activism going?"

"Do I look like the kind of guy who starts petitions on the internet?"

"Depends if it was to increase the height of doors."

Will stayed cool after his joke, so Angelina had to do the same. Hobson laughed, but only a disappointed chuckle. "Right. So you've got nothing?"

"I don't know, Hobson. Considered setting traps? You could get a pneumatic drill, dig a bear pit?"

Hobson stared back at him, not giving any clues on his thoughts at first. In the end, though, a small grin sneaked out.

"Interesting idea, Will. I'll think about it."

"I wasn't being serious."

"Doesn't mean you weren't right. Come on, Choi. Work to do." He went for the exit, stamping his feet, and punched the door release so hard it crunched. Angelina found herself alone facing Will.

"Is he about to dig a bear pit to catch chuggers?" Will asked, a smile playing around his lips.

"Hard to tell. So, um, good to see you again."

"Yeah. Thanks for retweeting my poem this morning."

"Oh, no worries, it was funny."

"And meaningful too, though. Thought it really said something about the plight of the modern desk minder."

"Oh yes, I thought it definitely..."

"Choi! Heel!" came the roar from the door. She did the wave again and quit that room while she was ahead, making sure not to look back.

By the time she made it outside, Hobson was a few huge steps back the way they'd come, excited into motion by whatever idea he'd had. Angelina went to follow, reaching a few metres clear of the Brightman when she heard dashing steps behind.

Oh God, had Will decided he *must* kiss her? Or was she about to be mugged then stabbed? Either way, couldn't stop herself turning round.

Turns out, it was neither of those things – just a man with dreadlocks in a green neon outfit. Hobson looked round, but not in time to save Angelina from the words she'd been dreading: "Excuse me, Miss, can you spare a few minutes to talk about Africa?"

TWELVE
SWEET CHARITY

"Yes? Can I help you?"

Angelina's whole body froze, she wasn't sure how her lips were moving.

"Do you know that thousands of children are dying in the third world every second?"

Well, she'd assumed kids were dying *somewhere*.

He was taller than her, white with big dreadlocks and a goatee. A beaded necklace was visible before the neon green anorak swept in to cover his clothes, shrouding him in brand identity. The matching clipboard with huge logo also drew focus from his face. Even charities didn't want to be too associated with hippies, Angelina thought. Still, she'd bet good money there was a multi-coloured home-dyed sack underneath that mac. Or perhaps she was hitting the stereotype bottle too hard.

"No, I didn't know that," she said, "although I kinda presumed, but... no."

Was that the right answer?

To her relief, the green man on the street didn't scythe into her apathy. "So are you interested in helping them out?"

"Oh, I don't have much money, I don't have a job, I'm on an unpaid work experience thing for him."

She gestured up the road at Hobson, leaning against a lamppost watching her struggle. Well, pretending to look at his phone, but glancing up every few seconds. For someone who claimed to hate chuggers, he didn't seem to mind his intern getting sucked into their guilty quicksand.

"Ah, right, well, does your employer want to make a regular donation, maybe?"

"I'm sure he does. Hey, Hobson," she called over to him, "are you interested?"

Even though he'd clearly been listening to their conversation, Hobson jumped like she'd thrown water in his face. "Say what?"

The flow of pedestrians took a marked detour around them now. Angelina, Hobson and the nameless street fundraiser occupied an oval-shaped island on the pavement. No-one else dared enter, too scared that dread clipboard would fire out suction cups to extract their bank account numbers.

People stepped gingerly around, all at the same insistent gentle angle. Eyes kept trained at either their feet or some unspecified vanishing point.

In that moment, she almost felt sorry for the clipboard-holding street veterans. After all, they were trying to achieve something good, in their way. Maybe people ignored them rather than fighting back because it was kinder than telling them where to go. Perhaps she and Hobson should be doing the same.

If only she thought of that before setting the boss on them. Unfortunately, he was already crashing his way over.

"Hey," Hobson waved at the man with the silly face-fuzz, not sure how he would react. "How can I help ya?"

"Uh, well," he began, quavering at Hobson's sheer size. "Your young associate seemed to think you might be interested in, um, some kind of charitable donation."

"Heh." Hobson caught Choi's eye just as it began to widen, mouth open slightly.

The passers-by slowed their stride, trying to keep in sight should a fight break out, but with enough distance to avoid being dragged in. People always did that around Hobson.

"I'm a small business owner, y'know mate," Hobson shrugged. "Times are tough. I do what I can."

"So you already donate to charity?" Definite glint in the anorak-man's eye.

"I told you, I'm just trying to get by."

"So are we, Mister Hobson, and so are all the people we're trying to help."

"You…" Hobson stopped talking halfway through a word and looked at Choi again. Glanced over his shoulder, imagining Bobby and The Pimp sitting outside that café, the owner waiting inside for people to pick up a single coffee. Shops putting out binbags, Rush Recruitment's slave workers praying to get through the day.

Hobson found himself staring at his feet. He looked back up to catch the chugger's eye.

"You might just be right."

"Does that mean you'll consider donating, sir?"

"Not a chance in hell, son. But good talking nonetheless."

"Okay then, sir. You too."

"Cheers then." Hobson turned and surged up the street, Choi scampering along after him. The small crowd dispersed, disappointed at the lack of combat. They ambled away this way and that, a couple looking after Hobson with eyes that screamed *'We recognise you from the internet!'*

They kept going, crossed the high street, glances still pouring into them. Since it was the nearest place to take cover, he led them into the same café as before, and thankfully it was empty. Passing morning trade dried up, wasn't quite lunchtime yet.

"Hey," Hobson called across the room to the counter, "what's your name?"

The barista was a middling-sized chap in an apron and wearing a thin layer of stubble. His reply sounded wary. "Jamie. That's why it's called *Jamie's Café*. Can I help you, sir?"

"Well, I'll need a word in a moment, but can I have a coffee first, and Choi?"

"Er, do you have any fruit tea infusions?" she said, looking like she was about to be hit by a truck.

"Certainly, madam, is lemon okay?"

She smiled. "That'd be great, thanks."

"I'll bring them over, take a seat."

So they sat down, choosing the corner furthest away from Jamie. Hobson leaned in as close to Choi as he could without making them both feel uncomfortable.

"So, I've had to refine it a bit, but I think I've settled on our fuckin' strategy to deal with this case. Wanna hear it?"

With obvious hesitation, she nodded.

"Don't worry, Choi," he tried a smile to put her at ease, "I think you're gonna like it. It's actually part-inspired by something you walked into earlier."

"Y'see, Jamie mate," Hobson began, as if he'd known the café barista for years rather than minutes. "We've had some complaints about these street fundraising chaps outside the station. It's annoying innit?"

Jamie was in the middle of serving a customer, and seemed unsure what to make of the enormous bloke sidling up to the end of his counter and letting rip. Angelina didn't want to tell Hobson how to speak unto his people, but why did he always play up the matey cockney *'Y'know mate innit'* vernacular when talking to a stranger?

The words hung there in space, spat out where they didn't quite fit.

"Can this wait a moment, sir?" said Jamie, at last. "I've just got to finish this lady's coffee."

"No worries." Hobson stepped back, holding up his hands to show he wasn't armed. Why this was necessary, Angelina dreaded to think.

So they stood at the end of the counter, waiting until Jamie was free. The customer was short, female. She gave Hobson the kind of nervy eyeball you'd expect for a weird bloke talking too loud. She had a woolly hat pulled down over a few wisps of blonde fringe and reminded Angelina of Emily Allen from Social Awesome. In fact, she ended up double taking to make sure it wasn't her.

That done, Angelina turned to Hobson, still hovering in the middle of the establishment. His every twitch said *'Just pretend I'm not here'*, despite his size making that impossible.

"Hobson, maybe I could handle this?" she said, trying not to flinch away.

"Hm?"

"Do you know this guy at all? Ever been in here before?"

"Not really, but Benny was here and I know you like these coffee shop things, so..."

"Exactly," Angelina leapt in, "I come to Starbucks and stuff all the time, I know the etiquette, let me at it."

She'd expected Hobson to need persuading, but it seemed not. He was back to their seat in the corner at amazing speed, knocking a chair over in his wake.

Angelina took a deep, calming breath. Best not fuck up now.

Jamie passed a steaming takeaway cup to the Emily lookalike. She bustled out of the café, carefully not looking at Hobson or Angelina. Another PR triumph.

"So, Jamie, hi," she said, doing the small wave.

"Hello," he gave her a big smile of glowing white teeth, then looked away again to clean the nozzle of his milk-frother. "What can I do you for? Another lemon tea?"

"Yes please," she smiled, "and also, my friend and I wanted to talk to you about the charity fundraising outside the station."

"Ah yes, he said." Jamie whipped her teabag into a mug. "I gather he doesn't like it?"

"No, he doesn't, he thinks it puts people off the area. We were wondering if you'd help us maybe do something about them?"

"Hm." Jamie put her prospective drink underneath an urn and hissed boiling water into it. "I'm not up for a fight."

"Don't worry." She found herself doing the hands-up-I'm-unarmed gesture now. "No violence. We just thought: you know how there's always bags of trash along the pavements round here? And I keep falling over them and it's *so* embarrassing?"

"Not our fault the council are useless, ma'am."

"Oh, I know, I know. But we just thought: since you've got the rubbish anyway, why not leave a few bags outside the station? If we get a few local businesses involved, we could have the place too stinky for the clipboard people to hang around."

As he plonked her drink onto a saucer, Jamie considered her proposition. A smile spread across his face, until he burst out laughing. "Interesting suggestion, certainly. Sorry, do you have a name?"

"I'm Angelina Choi, and that's John Hobson."

Jamie took a long, considered gaze at them both, before turning back to his machines. "Never heard of either of you."

"Don't worry, I didn't expect…" She checked on Hobson, watching them from his corner, before lowering her voice. "Do you not know him at all? Because Hobson acts like he's some kind of local hero and his old office is just across the road."

Jamie stopped rattling his crockery and came over to the segment of bar where Angelina stood, leaning in to speak quietly. He checked out Hobson again on the way down. "Never heard of him, but I know those people he was in with earlier."

"Benny and The Pimp?"

"Yeah. Maybe they've got good hearts, but they're not exactly straight and narrow guys. So, I dunno," Jamie shrugged, "maybe he's just a friend of the not-quite-conventional."

"You mean criminals?"

"I ain't assuming anything. Maybe your boss is a Peckham folk legend and I'm not *with it* enough to know."

"I guess."

Jamie reached into his pocket and pulled out a small card with *Jamie's Café* and the shop details on it, including his mobile number. Considering how plain the rest of the joint was, it was nicely designed. Minimalist, intricate patterns weaving up the side. As she turned it over in her hand, he said, "Give me a call when you've sorted out this plan, okay?"

"Sure." She pocketed the card and threw him a smile. "Thanks Jamie."

"Any time, ma'am."

He seemed like a nice man, Angelina thought as she walked back towards Hobson with her tea. Looked in his thirties, so about ten years too old to like *in that way*, but a good guy nonetheless. She hoped Hobson's plan wouldn't screw him over somehow.

"Hi," she said as she sat back down.

"Choi," he grinned. "Looking victorious there. Is he in?"

"Think so. Gave me his card to let him know the details. What next?"

"Three or four shops and we're sorted."

"Cool." Angelina giggled. "Is this not punishing the commuters who have to walk through the smell, though?"

"Hey, they can walk straight off," Hobson fired back, "but the chuggers hang around the station for hours. They're fucked."

"Fair enough."

"There is one small flaw in our plan, though," he admitted after a pause. "Benny may not be thrilled to hear he has to do his preaching through a fog of shit-stench."

"Ah."

"Thing is, Benny," Hobson began, knowing he only had once chance to get this right. "You don't want us to resort to violence against these chugging folk, right? Cos after all, they're just trying to get on with their day, no need to do anything too drastic?"

"No," Benny shook his head firmly, "that's the last thing I could ever want."

"Good, okay," he said, ignoring Choi's smugging to his left. They were sat on a bench outside Subway, each carrying their own bag emitting the standard smell all Subway sandwiches made. That processed factory-preserved aroma that reminded you it was all becoming the same.

Choi found it unappetising – for him, the reliable familiarity was part of the charm. Still, she was eating her sandwich, taking care not to spill any sauce down her blouse. Served her right for ordering it in the first place.

They'd grabbed Benny on his lunchbreak, so he was wearing his good work clothes, smiling, sometimes waving to passing strangers. Local people really seemed to love him. Hobson couldn't tell if he felt impressed or jealous.

"So, we have a plan – we think the local shop owners are pretty sick of the chuggers too. So we persuade them to dump a few trash bags outside the station, stink the place out, the pests stop going there. Sound good?"

Benny burst out laughing, a deep, throaty, joyous noise. "That is good justice, sir!"

"Uh-huh. So listen, we've asked around and had some interest. Still, one problem: if you wanna stay there, you'll be stuck preaching in the smell too."

"I see."

Benny gazed away, but the smile never left his face. "Mister Hobson, Jesus Christ had nails forced through his hands, I think I can handle a little odour."

"You sure, mate? It's gonna be pretty rank, we've got the fishmonger involved and everything."

"I happen to adore seafood. One question, though: is this not illegal? Dumping rubbish wherever you like?"

"It kinda is." Hobson gazed into his meatball sub and thought about Ellie last night. "But community spirit, y'know? We pull together and they can't touch us. These days, the police don't care about anyone but the rich. They ain't gonna launch an investigation. It'll be the council or something, and who gives a shit, y'know?"

Benny nodded and flashed another pearly white grin. "Excellent."

"Settled, then." Hobson finished off his lunch, dunking the wrapping into the bin next to the bench, and got up. "Choi, let's go. Gonna sort out a schedule with the shopkeepers, then head back to our office. No point hanging around here."

She looked up in the middle of a bite. "What?"

"You heard. We'll check back later, but this ain't urgent enough or paying enough to sit around for hours. See you round, Benny. Hopefully we'll get this sorted for you."

"Much appreciated, Mister Hobson."

And he was gone. Hobson had to admit, the ragged, shouting lunatic from the station looked damned weird wearing a sharp suit.

"Okay, Choi," he laughed as she choked trying to finish her sandwich. "You stay there for a sec, I'm just going to head inside and ask the manager of Subway if he'll shove his crap outside the station too."

"So, um, what you said to Benny about the police – you're really just counting on Ellie letting us off again, right?"

Angelina had spent the journey back to the Inspiration Gestation Station plucking up the courage to ask that. Before, they discussed their street-littering plan and made snide observations about fellow passengers. They were in sight of the IGS by the time she managed it.

"If necessary," he said, not as complacently as when they'd broken into the supermarket. "But I doubt it'll come to that, Choi. The cops don't care about this shit, especially when it affects chuggers. All we need is them to pull out of our street and job done. We're not trying to ruin any lives here."

"Right. You know it's not *our* street? We don't work there anymore?"

"You know I mean," he grumbled.

By now, they were at the door of the IGS, holding their card against the lock and stepping back into the pastoral entrance.

"Afternoon, guys," Jacq said, smiling out behind the desk, "how's it going? Any good cases?"

"Not bad, Jacq." Hobson gave her a nod. "In fact, this one's almost fun, thank fuck. I was getting tired of all the blood and moaning."

"That's nice," Jacq said, looking thrilled. "You have a guest upstairs, by the way."

"And you just let them in? Again?" Hobson's relaxed tone choked up with gravel. "I know you're not exactly a born fighter, but let's have *some* security. Who is it?"

Jacq sounded crestfallen. "I thought it'd be okay, it's only Lettie."

"Lettie Vole?" Hobson said, looking back at Angelina. "Choi, ain't she your mate? Are you two going out in Dalston after work to drink cocktails from teacups and paint stripes on your faces?"

"I… What? No," Angelina spluttered out eventually, "I don't know why she's here."

"Glorious. Alright then, thanks Jacq."

At his gruff tone, Jacq's face fell even further.

But no time for Angelina to give her a hug, as Hobson surged into the lift and punched the button.

Soon enough, they emerged from the lift. Through the window, Angelina spotted Lettie sat behind her own former desk, hair a dirtier shade of red than normal. She looked weak and colourless, like she hadn't been sleeping. Her clothes – formal shirt and trousers – were cleaner than her face and hands. So she dressed up for this visit, but still didn't bother washing.

Rather than using her phone to keep busy while she waited, Lettie kept staring at the office doors until they opened.

"Angie!" she smiled without much joy, mouth pulling tightly back. "How are you?"

"I'm…" Angelina struggled, conscious of Hobson watching her. "I'm okay, Lettie. What's wrong?"

"Oh, um, I need a hand actually. Some help. May even need to hire you."

Angelina froze up at that, so Hobson stabbed into the conversation. "Nice t'see you Lettie. Help with what?"

"Well, it's not so much me as Pete." She stared at him. "Pete needs help."

"Right, well." Hobson looked away. "Unless he wants help fucking off and leaving me alone, I can't see him getting it."

He went to storm back to his office, but Angelina couldn't let him do it. Lettie looked so sad.

So, almost certain it was a bad idea, Angelina opened up the whole can of worms. After all, she and Lettie were almost friends, before her brother being a serial killer made things awkward. To be fair to Pete, his sister exacerbated the problem by later killing someone herself.

"What does Pete need help with, Lettie? I can't promise anything, but... y'know."

THIRTEEN
IT BITES BACK

As Violet Vole turned towards him, Hobson felt his leg twinge. Thanks to constant hammering painkillers, it hadn't stung much in the last few days. But her green eyes burrowing into his dead grey ones brought the inconvenient pain flooding back.

Choi stared at him too, wearing the same begging expression. At least they both remembered who *The Talent* at this agency was, Hobson thought. They could moan about morality all they wanted, but still needed him on board. Choi asked Lettie to tell them her problem, but all a waste of time until he agreed to listen.

Leaning back against one of the many vacant desks, Hobson fixed Lettie with a stare. Gave her the most distant nod he could manage.

"Go on then," he said. "What does Pete need help with? Is Edward Lyne's cousin sending him abusive messages on Twitter?"

Lettie shivered in her seat, eye contact dropped. Good, Hobson thought. He'd feel ashamed too if that ratty little scrote were his brother.

In the end, though, her face reset into the usual hard fury.

"Well," she began, "you know that dog he was using?"

"You mean the huge angry wolfhound thing with the teeth and claws that he was setting on people, including *me?*"

She ground her teeth before answering. "Yes, Mister Hobson. That one. You know he stole it from his neighbour?"

"Uh-huh."

"Yalin Makozmo, some kind of underground dogfighting trainer?"

"I'm aware of that guy, yeah," Hobson said. "Although in your idiot brother's defence, he only stole the thing after it killed Makozmo and legged it."

"Yeah, um, turns out the fucking criminal underworld don't see it that way." Lettie leant forward, looking more herself with every swearword. "He's been getting threats in his cell. They say it's his fault the twats lost their dog *and* have the police up their arses."

Never occurred to Hobson the cops would ask Pete where he found the murder weapon, never mind look into it further. Why couldn't they take his word for everything and go for a donut?

"Right. So what d'you want me to do about it? Buy them another dog?"

"Hobson," Choi hissed from behind him. He'd almost forgotten she was there. "Be nice."

"Look, I..." Lettie dropped her eyes again. "My family are well off, you saw our house. We'll pay you to help, give you any bribe money they want, whatever. He says they're threatening to kill him, they've tried once already but the police stopped it. Eventually, they'll succeed. Help us save him, please. I know he's crazy and shit, but we don't want him to die."

She slumped back into her seat, Hobson stared out of the window. Helping clients was fine, but serial killers in distress? Did he want to get involved?

"Choi," he said, at last, "can I have a word?"

She and Lettie exchanged baffled looks. "Yes?"

"Okay." He pointed over to his office, the only private space they had. "In there, then."

They weaved around the desks towards the corner box, Hobson turning back to the angry visitor as they went. "Oh, try not to kill anyone while I'm gone, okay?"

She averted her eyes for a moment before nodding. Jesus, it was just a joke.

Hobson switched the lights on and dropped his bulk into the desk chair with a heavy sigh. Once settled, he opened his eyes and looked right at Angelina.

"Okay Choi, you reckon we should take the case?"

"Come again?"

He shrugged. "I heard what she wants, I ain't sure, I'm asking your opinion. You know this Vole family, do we want to get involved with them again?"

Angelina emitted an umming noise resembling a broken radio while she chewed it over. She recognised the lonely desperation in the woman outside's voice. It sounded dangerous, much like Lettie herself. Could they trust her?

"I... I mean, can we do it? Do you have a plan?"

"Ain't much planning to do. Find the twats, ask them to back off. If they want paying, get the family to cough up. If they won't, lean on the cops. End of plan."

"I see." Angelina looked out through the slightly ajar door of Hobson's office. Lettie was staring at her own hands, trying not to peek at them too often. "And you know where we can find the twa... people?"

"Got a decent idea."

"Okay."

Catching Angelina's eye, Lettie abandoned nonchalance and gave her the full-on sad eyes. Hobson watched Angelina too, motionlessly waiting for her expert opinion.

So she rolled her neck back and looked at the ceiling instead, which didn't expect much of her. Standing there, hands in her pockets, head slack and eyes fixed upwards, well aware she looked like an idiot.

At least they were *saving someone* this time, the case seemed the right thing to do, and Hobson made it sound possible. Felt like something *must* go wrong, but was that just self-doubt? No choice but to ignore it if she ever wanted someone like Hobson to respect her. If she even did.

Jesus.

"Alright then." She took in Lettie as she looked back down, before landing on Hobson. "I guess I say we take the case, then. If you want my opinion."

"I asked, didn't I? Stop doubletalking yourself, it's annoying."

Angelina laughed. "Sorry. So we're doing it?"

"Why not? Could always use the money, and we did kinda get her into it. Let's go."

Hobson got up and headed back out into the office. Angelina let him go first.

"Alright, Vole," Hobson said as they emerged, clapping his hands. "Good news: we're taking your case."

Lettie's whole face smiled. "Thanks, Mister Hobson, it means a lot. I'm sure my family will…"

Brushing past her with a tut, Hobson gestured towards the lift. "Save it for your gushing quote to the papers."

"Fine." As Angelina passed, Lettie turned to tap her on the shoulder. "Hey, Angie, thanks."

"Why?"

Lettie giggled before answering. "Oh, y'know. Thought you might've talked the big man into it."

"Don't call him that when he's in earshot, for God's sake."

Lettie laughed again, but still looked over to check Hobson was far away. "Hey, you didn't tell him about… um, me killing Edward Lyne, did you?"

"No. I didn't think it would help anyone."

"Cool. Exactly fucking right. Let's go, then." She grinned and dashed along to the lift.

Angelina couldn't help trailing her feet as she followed. Got there in the end, though.

"So, where are we going?" Lettie asked Hobson as the three of them crowded into the bright metal box.

"You're coming, are you?"

"Can I not?" She said that without a hint of doubt. Even though she knew Lettie had problems, Angelina felt a flash of envy.

"If you must. We're hitting our least favourite place in the world, Lettie. The Left Hand, wankstained pub of crime, where Makozmo used to take his scary beasts."

"Shitting hell."

Angelina nodded in silent agreement.

Things fell quiet. Stayed that way until they were passing the reception desk again and Jacq couldn't resist a nervous hello. "Everything alright, guys?"

"Not bad," Hobson gruffed.

"And everything was... okay with Lettie going up?"

Angelina saw him draw in a mouthful of air to unleash some sharp retort, but it never reached the outside world. Indeed, he sounded quite upbeat: "Everything's fine, Jacq. Don't worry about it. See you later, yup?"

"You bet!" The glee snapped back in place. Angelina began to find Jacq's cheeriness annoying – oddly, just as Hobson himself seemed to be warming up to her.

"Fuck me," Lettie said, a few seconds after they walked into The Left Hand.

"Yeah, wouldn't say that so loud," Hobson muttered, not quick enough to stop the first *"If you insist, darling"* drifting over from a nearby table. He counted four guys in hole-punctured hoodies slumped over pints, and at only four in the afternoon.

"Wow, I see what you mean," Lettie murmured back to him once they'd passed the heckler's table. "This place is awful."

"Oh, that was standard bad-pub stuff. You gotta start going to worse bars," Hobson said. "The shady part is up the back."

Choi eyed up the dark mire at the top of the room, keeping quiet and no doubt repressing everything. She'd moan about the scummy clientele later, he knew, but fine. Just don't whine while they're in earshot.

At the other end of the scale, Lettie Vole fidgeted and glanced everywhere. "Christ," she breathed, "any good stuff?"

"Jesus fuck, will you shut up?" Hobson growled as they reached the bar.

The goatee-wearing barman looked less happy to see him every time. Wasn't late enough in the day yet for the place to be full, so the three of them stuck out. Hobson because he was massive, the other two just for being women – although the Asian teenager was a particularly sore thumb.

"What'll it be this time, sir? Would you like to set up a tab?"

"I'm fine. Pint of the Noddy Shark," Hobson gestured at one of the ale taps, "and a coffee for my junior partner…"

"I still don't like coffee," Choi leapt in.

"Make that a glass of tap water, or toilet water if you got any. Lettie?"

"Coke please. But the soft drink, not…"

"Yeah, he gets it, cheers."

The barman gave Hobson another sad *'Why can't you just piss off?'* look, before going to get their drinks.

"Sorry," Lettie murmured, "I thought since this was a dodgy pub, he might think I meant, you know, *coke.*"

"Yeah, don't know how often you've bought drugs, Lettie," Hobson said, as calm as he could, "but the codes are normally a little harder to crack."

"Sorry," she said, again.

"Keep it together, for fuck's sake. Choi's doing better than you and she's about ten."

"Thanks," Choi mumbled.

The barman came back and crashed their drinks down in front of them, splashing beer all around. Hobson turned over a tenner, got most of it back, and they made for the dark, abandoned back end of the pub.

This was where the regulars talked bad shit. He met Micro there last week and avoided it on his return visit with Rocky yesterday. Normally, it was empty, rows of vacant tables daring non-scumbags to sit there. Even when the pub was full last night, most punters never found the courage to sit at those tables.

This time, though, the allocated crime area was occupied. Before Hobson and company could investigate, the waddling form of Micro loomed into view, slapping a soggy jacket potato in front of a despondent customer. It oozed liquid carb before she even poked it with her fork.

As the Left Hand's kitchen king groaned his way upright, he saw them and splashed over.

"Micro," Hobson said, trying not to recoil.

"Hobson. Looking for anyone special?"

"Maybe."

"Because the Polish gentlemen at the back have been asking after you ever since you caught that guy with the dog." He pointed towards the crowd. "I did try to tell you last night, but you seemed to be…"

Hobson nodded and marched into the murk without wasting another word. A group of identical shaven-headed guys in tracksuits gathered around one of the sticky tables, deep in conversation. They looked over as soon as Hobson stomped into their dark space and he didn't recognise a single one.

"Mister Hobson," said the tallest chap in the

darkest, shiniest sportswear – did that count as a suit in these circles? Hobson's usual black jacket and tie felt like formalwear right now.

"Afternoon," Hobson said.

As the apparent leader rose from the dark to stand, Hobson realised this guy wasn't in a good way. A huge scar ran from one end of his lips up to the ear, as if someone tried to open up his face. When he spoke, his mouth moved unnaturally on that side, skin pulling tight around the cut.

His bald head wasn't polished to a smooth shine like a TV villain, but speckled with stubble and scabs, like the surface of the moon. Either terrible at shaving or suffering chronic radiation sickness.

"So," he continued in a strong accent, "what brings you here? Speak quickly, we are trying to have lunch."

His bald clone army didn't have any food in front of them, but seemed put out by Hobson's presence nonetheless. The boss had a full microwaved roast dinner ready to go. Looked much better than that jacket potato.

"Yeah, okay. What's your name, mate?"

"Joseph is fine."

"Hi, Joseph. You wouldn't know Yalin Makozmo?"

The maimed face of the boss twitched, as if trying to frown, but stopped by the tight scar. "Yes. He was my nephew."

"Balls. So you'll be the people trying to kill Pete Vole over Yalin's dog, then?"

"Yes."

A moment later, Lettie Vole yelled out from behind him. Something about fucking Polish motherfuckers, maybe a racist jab about Communism. The other guys, the muscle or whatever, joined

Joseph in rising to their feet.

Looking over his shoulder in a self-conscious moment, Hobson saw the swingdoors to the kitchen drift on their hinges. The huge shoulders of Micro shuddered against them, head perched inside the square window. Big chubby grin, definitely enjoying the show. Motherfucker.

"Look, guys," Hobson said, "she's Vole's sister, she's just a bit annoyed about someone trying to kill her brother. Considering you're doing this over family, you understand, yeah?"

Mostly got blank stares, but the boss gave a small nod.

"Apologise," Hobson said to Lettie, snapping the word without any room for negotiation.

"What? Fuck off."

"Do it," he growled, "or they'll kill all three of us and the chef will cook us into his sausages."

"He's not joking," Choi added.

Lettie gave a cold look to them both, before turning it on the Polish gangsters. She grunted out *"Sorry, I'm just very upset,"* with dead eyes. It was pathetic, but she projected such an air of humiliation, Joseph seemed satisfied.

"Okay, look, enough," Hobson said, "let's get down to business. We want you to leave Pete Vole be, what'll it take? The family have money."

Joseph stepped around the table and underlings to stand up in front of Hobson. There was a definite smell of dry scabs.

"You caught Peter Vole. You are responsible for the police crawling all over us. You have worked for Rush Recruitment. We'll take you instead."

Hobson laughed, not on purpose. "Joseph, look,

I'm here to work this out, yeah, but ain't gonna stand here and let you kill me."

"Not kill you. You have experience from your past work. Do a job for us, we let this go."

John Hobson closed his eyes and inhaled. This was not contributing to his redemption in the way he'd hoped. He looked over at Choi, but her face was blank. Joseph, on the other hand, was giving him more and more eyeball.

Never taking a case to keep a teenage girl happy again. He meant it this time.

FOURTEEN
EXCUSES, EXCUSES

"Don't worry, Mister Hobson, we will not be asking you to kill anyone." Joseph's voice sounded like he thought he was being benevolent. Hobson readied himself for disaster.

"Oh good."

"No, you are just helping us smuggle some drugs."

"Even better."

"So, meet us back here tomorrow morning for the pick-up?"

Hobson sometimes struggled to feel much moral outrage on the narcotics issue. On the scale of bad things, he'd seen real evil meted out to unwilling victims – violence, imprisonment, worse. In comparison, sale of opiates to enthusiastic customers felt like a drop in the ocean.

But as he grew older, the world closed in for him. Did a junkie yearn for smack as much as Hobson wanted to stop trying and do whatever the fuck was easiest? Maybe, he'd concluded whilst drunk a few months back, it wasn't as simple as he used to think.

Nonetheless, he still felt a definite surge of relief that the big job was *'just drugs'*, meaning he didn't have to crush the life out of anyone with his bare hands. It came out as one huge calming sigh. Kept him floating through a polite goodbye to Joseph and his men. Out of the pub, down the road and towards the station, ignoring the ratty shops.

After that, though, the gnawing in his gut returned.

"Okay," he turned to Choi and Lettie, "I'm sending you two on a job."

"Yes?" said Choi.

"I don't work for you?" said Lettie.

"Don't care. Go to Markham Road, talk to Ric McCabe, look around again, see if you can spot *anything* I can use to get out of this."

"Like what?"

"If he's seen any bald scumbags breaking the law outside his house, that'd be a fucking good start."

Choi started to open her mouth again, as if about to question the point of the errand. Their eyes met, she looked away. "Come on, Lettie. We can walk from here."

"Fuck Markham Road, Angie."

The two women were standing at the end of the street next to the sign, looking up the tarmac. Darkness was dropping, Angelina growing cold – soon, she must insist Lettie get a move on. People passed by, stepping faster to get away from the swearing loiterers.

Still, Lettie looked deep in thought as she slouched against that wall. It felt heartless to rush her.

"What do you mean, Lettie?"

"I mean, I guess..." She looked up the street again, towards the house where Peter Vole, Eric McCabe and William Lane once lived together – at least, until her brother turned out to be a serial killer and set a dog on one of the others, followed by several more people. Angelina shuddered, Lettie continued. "You reckon it wouldn't have happened if he hadn't lived here?"

"You think you could've saved him from his own craziness by not letting him leave home?"

"I mean," Lettie turned back to Angelina, eyes wide and tears forming, "if he hadn't moved in next to Makozmo and his stupid dog, if he'd not had the opportunity to steal the fucking beast, would he have never done it? Or would he have found a way anyway?"

"I don't know, Lettie. I try not to think about that stuff too much."

"Heh." Lettie laughed, it came out choked. "You're icy for a kid, anyone ever tell you that?"

"A few times. Have you not been here since it happened?"

"No. Had a few emails from Ric, used to be kinda friendly with him back in the day, but didn't reply."

"Are you sure you want to do this now, then?"

"Yeah. Should try and help, I suppose." Lettie thrust herself up from the wall with her hips. Still not pulling her hands out of her coat pockets, she pushed off towards her brother's old house. "Come on, let's do this. Don't want Hobson to think we're not pulling our weight."

Thank fuck for that. Angelina fell into step with Lettie.

When Ric opened the door to his house, Angelina couldn't stop herself laughing out-loud. Even Lettie looked down at her feet to suppress a smile.

He waited for them to finish, grumbling. "Yes, thanks, I'm aware it hasn't quite worked out."

"Sorry. You look like a cartoon lemon." Angelina hadn't really laughed for a few hours, so let herself enjoy this one. After previous experiments in red and black, his hair was bright yellow, like sweetcorn or a well-ripened banana. Other than that, he was wearing an unwashed black hoodie and torn jeans, clearly not expecting company.

"Fuck me, Ric." Lettie was more amused than hysterical, but it was a start. "Why haven't you re-dyed it something less stupid?"

"It was only a couple of hours ago. I was going to run out and buy more dye in a bit."

"Wearing a hat, I assume." Angelina grinned.

"Yeah, yeah." As ever, his world-weary expression was exaggerated for maximum drama. "What can I do for you two?"

"We wanted a word, if that's okay," she said, pushing her lips horizontal. "About the murders and the dog and stuff."

"Okay," Ric pulled the door fully open and waved towards his living room. "In you come."

They stepped inside, mumbling their thanks. Saddened back into silence by the mention of the murders, they filed through Ric's hallway in silence. The sitting area remained a filthy hole, illuminated only by a single unshaded light bulb. The number of abandoned, sauce-streak-stained plates had spiralled, probably because Ric had no housemates left to clean up after him.

The sole remaining resident dropped into an armchair, letting the other two share a grey-brown sofa. Dust kicked up from both. "So what do you want to know?" he said, after a conspicuous gap.

Angelina nudged Lettie. This was her case, she may as well speak. Getting the message, Violet Vole took a deep breath.

"So the Polish mafia or whatever are threatening to shank Pete in prison because he got their dog killed and the police are onto them now. Apparently they'll let it go if Hobson helps them with..." A glance at Angelina. "Something, but we wondered if you saw anything we could, like, use against them? I don't think Hobson really wants to do crime for me."

"Right." Ric's face became paler in the sickly cheap light, which only made his hair look more ridiculous. "Um, not sure I got much. This may come as a shock to you both, but I tend to look the other way if I suspect I'm witnessing organised crime. I'm very British like that. If Hobson can sort it, why don't we just let him?"

The three of them sat in Ric's living room, looking at each other, letting the atmosphere thicken. Angelina's eyes narrowed and she leaned forward to get Ric's full attention. "Look, it's not fair to force Hobson to do this just because you're fucking scared. Do you know anything or not?"

A tense silence followed, broken only by Lettie chuckling. When everyone looked at her, all she said was: "Sorry, I just like it when Angie swears."

Angelina kept glaring at Ric, determined not to let him off.

At long last, he exhaled. "Okay, why the fuck not, I might have something. Gonna need a drink first though, you two ladies want to join me? It's been hard to use up the booze since both my housemates fucked off."

"Um, yeah," Angelina said, dumbfounded by her own success. "If you like."

"Fuck off!" Hobson yelled, sending another file sailing out of his office and into the small pile gathering on the floor outside.

For hours, Hobson combed through Edward Lyne's old paperwork, trying to find anything related to this Joseph guy and his little gang. Plenty of material on Rush Recruitment, worrying amount on Hobson's past, not much on the Left Hand and its dogfighting scene.

No news from Choi and Lettie either. Now he'd taken the gig, he was reluctant to quit, but did he really need to become a drug mule?

Yelling alone wasn't as relaxing as Hobson anticipated. He could call Tony for a pint, but after last night's snippy attitude, drinking with his main friend wasn't as appealing as usual.

Instead, he picked up the internal line and spoke to his only convenient acquaintance.

"Hey, um, Jacq. You alright? Yeah, listen, sorry I snapped at you earlier."

She seemed happy to hear that.

"Good. So, I've got time to kill, do you want to grab some booze and come have a couple when you finish? I'll drink anything as long as it's beer."

"So, Lettie, you still all about the red wine?" Ric hovered the bottle over a glass as he asked.

"Yes, thanks," Lettie said, not sounding gracious.

"And Miss Choi – I assume you'll be wanting a sugary alcopop?"

"Why, do you have one?" Angelina hated herself for sounding excited. Still, she only drank at friends' houses and that *was* her usual tipple.

"No. But I do have orange juice, vodka and a bag of icing sugar. Back in a moment."

Ric disappeared into his kitchen. A noise like a small car crash sounded when he stepped through the door, plates and cutlery sliding over each other. Despite her continuing sulk, a smile slipped onto Lettie's face.

The house fell quiet again after that, only clinking glasses and sucking thuds of the fridge door. Lettie splayed backwards on the sofa, whilst Angelina leaned forward, still tense.

"So what do you think he knows?" she asked, in her quietest audible voice.

"No fuckin' idea," Lettie said, "but if he can help keep my brother alive, I'll play along."

"Even though your brother killed your boyfriend?"

"Apparently so. And he wasn't my boyfriend."

"Right."

Angelina took her correction and fell silent again. She could see why Lettie might be in favour of forgiving murderers.

Ric returned, big smile and stupid hair just where they always were. He wielded a half-pint glass of red wine and another one containing a bright-coloured orange liquid.

"There we are, ladies. I'll just grab my beer." He seized one of the two cans lined up on the kitchen worktop. "Then I'll drink one of them, *then* we'll get started."

"Good." Angelina tried to keep businesslike, even as she took a sip of her orange stuff. It went right down her throat, sweetness overpowering her tastebuds, a warm kick floating up in its wake.

To give Ric his credit, this wasn't a bad approximation of an alcopop.

Even lift doors opened quieter when Jacq Miller used them. She just existed delicately. As such, Hobson didn't notice her arrival until she'd made it through the fire door into his company space, crept up to the entrance into his private cave and skirted around the discarded paperwork he'd hurled out there.

He wasn't doing anything embarrassing, just reading a file at his desk. Still, if he'd known company was here, might've done his flies and top shirt buttons back up. Maybe even slipped his jacket on.

Instead, she caught him kicked back in full relaxation mode. Luckily, he wasn't the type to blush easily. He dropped the cardboard sleeve onto his desk and stood up.

"Jacq, hi," he said, trying the warmest smile he could, lest he scare her off like a skittish woodland creature. "You done already?"

"Ah, yeah, the scheduled closing time is at seven, it's now quarter past."

She tapped her thick leather watchstrap as if to demonstrate the time. It matched everything else she wore – fabrics and wool, rather than harsh plastics or metal. Even the watchface itself was half-buried under strapping.

"Nice. And you brought... most of the off-licence?" He gestured towards her right hand, where a clinking carrier bag dangled. The tendons in her arm strained to keep it up; looked like nine or ten bottles, including two of wine.

"Well," she said, shrugging. "I wasn't sure what you'd like. So there's about four different things."

"Oh, I follow the whole fucking beer genre, it's fine." He waved his hand towards the many empty tables. "Put it down for God's sake, we ain't got a space problem."

Like a slow crane, she lowered the bag of glass onto a table. A deep sigh of relief escaped her lips as the weight left her.

Jacq flapped her arms, as if unsure what to do with them now. "So, um, what are you up to?" she said at last. Then she indicated the splayed-out folders in front of his office. "Having a clear-out? Are these old case files?"

"I'm... I'm trying to get out of a job, I think. Y'know how it is, you say you'll do something for someone, then realise it's shit."

"You mean like doing some DIY?"

"I... No." Hobson wasn't sure whether this was endearing or infuriating. "Not quite like that. Fuckin' hate DIY."

"You gotta try and take some satisfaction from whatever good comes from it, anyway. That's what I find." She smiled like a proud toddler.

"Come again?"

"Well, y'know," she said, speaking slower. "I'm a massive pushover, I'll do anything for anyone who asks. I'm not even sure why I'm up here now, but it makes me feel good so I try not to worry about the inconvenience."

"So you think I should just stop whining, smuggle the drugs and worry about the consequences later? 'Cause it'll make Lettie happy?"

Hobson hadn't meant to tell Jacq about the drugs, but he enjoyed the way her eyes doubled in size as she processed that word. Her feet shifted in place, until he burst out laughing. "Good Christ, sit down. There's plenty of tables, pick your favourite."

"Thanks." She shrank down behind her friend Emily's old desk, looking relieved she could no longer pace.

"Now," Hobson mused, "want to drink your wine from a mug or straight outta the bottle?"

The problem with alcopops, whether shopbought or homemade: they're dangerously easy to drink compared to their alcoholic strength. The sugar sends it slipping down the hatch, and before you even let go of your bottle, the room starts swimming.

Even worse, Angelina Choi wasn't an experienced drinker. She sat on the sofa, cradling the glass in her arms because there was nowhere to put it down. Must remember she was working still.

Not that you'd know it from Ric's big laughs and Lettie's content smiles. Part of her was reluctant to get in there and shut the chatter down – after all, it was the first time she'd seen Violet Vole have fun since her brother was jailed.

"So I went to a job interview with the green hair, right, and it was great. They could barely look at my face the entire time," Ric yelled, volume rising with every drink. "It was like being a woman with enormous tits, only the other way up. Maybe I should try shaving my head and getting it tattooed to look like a breast, would that work?"

Lettie cracked, laugh-snorting. "Ric, dear, you don't need to look any more of a tit than you already do."

RUSH JOBS

They raised their glasses to each other in a mock toast. All of a sudden, Angelina felt like a third wheel.

"So, um, guys, Ric," she hesitated out, "before you get too drunk, what was it you wanted to tell us about the dog and the Polish mob?"

"Oh yeah," Ric nodded, smile wavering a little. "I saw something. I should tell you, but you won't say you got it from me, will you? Didn't even tell the cops, I'm still pretty scared of those bald fuckers."

"Of course," Angelina said. Lettie nodded for emphasis.

"Okay," Ric said, sighing, hands clasped around his glass. "Yalin Makozmo was actually an okay guy. I mean, I know he tortured animals or whatever, but at least he was friendly. But his mates who came round to visit him, they were much more the type you'd expect. And more than once, right, I saw them holding dogs down in the back garden and shoving something down their throat. Then clamping their jaws shut, I guess so they had to swallow."

"What was it?" Angelina said, eyes wide.

"I... don't pretend to be an expert in crime," he mumbled, Lettie chuckled again. "But if you put a gun to my head, I'd say it was packages of drugs."

Angelina thought about what they'd asked Hobson to do and said: *"Fucking hell."*

The booze was disappearing fast back at the office. Hobson was feeling a little dizzy, to be honest, and Jacq was still going. She'd run out of wine and grabbed one of the beers he hadn't yet started.

He was less heavyweight than he used to be, and Jacq could drink a damn sight more than he expected. He gulped. The room wasn't exactly spinning, but Hobson felt vulnerable. Like the wrong part of his head was at the controls.

"I dunno, truth is, I was trying not to do this kinda shit anymore, and this… I feel like I'm being forced back into it, y'know?" Somewhere at the back of his mind, Hobson's dignity was wailing for mercy. At least he wasn't crying. "This sounds fuckin' childish, but it doesn't seem fair."

"At least you're doing it for a good reason." Jacq smiled. "I don't think Lettie's brother should die. And just the fact you're considering this stuff tells me you're a decent guy. You should feel okay."

Hobson didn't remember the movement, but they ended up sitting at the same desk finishing their drinks. Couldn't pick out the exact moment she leaned over and kissed him either, but he felt like quite the modern-day superhero by then. Why not, he supposed?

FIFTEEN
THAT MORNING

When Angelina woke up, alarm blazing across the room, she was immediately disgusted with herself.

Not because she'd done anything regrettable, simply for falling asleep on Ric's sofa. No way it wasn't crawling with disease. She peeled her face up, tossed the cushion away and wiped fingers down over her eyes. The floating cloud of brownness blanketing the living room only seemed heavier with sun wafting through it.

Plenty of stained, half-finished drinks left around the room, but no Ric or Lettie. She flicked off the alarm, swung her legs onto the ground and tried to sweep the creases out of her trousers. This was not pleasant. On the bright side, no terrified voicemails or texts from her mum, so she must've passed on an excuse for disappearing overnight.

She considered rummaging through the kitchen to find breakfast, but her muscles couldn't let her. It would be *stealing*, not to mention she'd probably contract a venereal condition from the tea towels.

It was nearly eight, anyway, and she had places to be. Angelina wondered if Lettie went upstairs to… *do* anything with Ric. Shuddering at the thought, she scanned her own mobile for clues.

Nothing from Lettie in her inbox, just this already-read message: *'Okay, thanks for letting me know at least, please do come home tomorrow. Mum.'*

So her mother still trying to seem cool and relaxed, then.

Out of curiosity, she went towards her Sent Messages to check out her excuse, but then her head fogged over with dim recollection. That wasn't all she'd transmitted last night.

Angelina remembered hovering over a *Send* button for ages, and she wouldn't dither like that without a good reason. Nothing in the texts except a bland missive to her Mum about staying over with Zoë. Blood pressure shooting, she rushed to her Facebook messages and found it: a transmission to Will, sent in the later hours of last night.

A sharp buzzing rising in her head, Angelina opened it up. *'Hi Will, back in Peckham tomorrow for work, wondered if you fancied meeting up for lunch? Xx'*

Two things sprang to mind: firstly, she never put kisses at the end of texts to anyone, never mind guys she barely knew. Second, that was eight hours ago, the fucking Facebook stalkprompt told her he'd read it not long after, *but no reply.*

"Shit," she hissed, just as Lettie staggered into the room to moan her agreement.

Hobson woke up just before his alarm sounded. His office was freezing cold – the Inspiration Gestation Station didn't heat itself to accommodate people crashing overnight.

His back roared with ache after sleeping slumped in an office chair out in the rank-and-file employee work area. Should've at least moved to his own more expensive seat. His eyes throbbed from sun bashing through the naked windows. His own coat lay over him, just about heavy enough to keep him warm. Despite his best efforts, he was spending the night at work more often than he'd like.

Then again, he thought as he spun the chair around, at least he hadn't been alone this time. Jacq was unconscious in one of the other chairs, leaning forward with her head on the desk and her own coat draped over her torso. Hobson was pretty sure he'd left that over her.

For a moment, he questioned whether they'd done anything else, but then he made to get up from the chair and felt a certain stickiness. Not to mention a used condom in the bin next to the chair, alongside various empty bottles.

Jacq got fully dressed before falling asleep, as far as he could see under that coat. Well, it was pretty cold out there. Hobson rubbed his temple and considered sneaking away.

Unfortunately, that option was ripped from him, as he hadn't bothered turning off the alarm. It rang out across the room, an awful shrill bleep, pushing his post-drinking headache into full awful motion.

Jacq stirred, mumbled, stretched an arm out like a cat, before realising this smooth, hard desk was not her mattress. She jolted upright as if it were red hot.

All this before she'd even seen Hobson, standing nearby rubbing his temples.

"Hi," he said, in a bid to head off awkward silences.

"Hello," she mumbled.

And then the quiet descended anyway.

"You alright?" he finally managed.

"Yes, think so. A bit sore from the desk. You?"

"Oh, y'know, I'm a detective, we're used to crashing in the office drunk." Casual shrug, attempt at a smile. "Just another day on the job. No big deal."

"Right, of course." She dropped eye contact. Hobson suspected he hadn't nailed this conversation.

She got up from the chair, straightened her trousers. Started mumbling about how she'd better get downstairs and start opening up. Barely time for him to shout a matey goodbye before Jacq disappeared through the door.

Hobson stared at the back of her head as she waited for the lift. He'd developed a certain respect for the woman, but she wasn't exactly his normal type. Didn't think she'd take certain human-trafficking aspects of his background well either.

Ugh.

In terms of not shitting where you eat, he'd done poor work here. Not just shat in the same restaurant, but directly onto his own plate.

She'd probably go to the bathroom and get cleaned up before putting herself out there on reception. This wasn't exactly a long-term solution, but if Hobson got off his arse now, he could make it out of the building without having to see her.

So that's exactly what he did.

"So, um, did you... y'know? With Ric?"

It took Angelina a few minutes of small talk to ask Lettie, but they were allegedly friends. She was sure *friends* talked about this kind of thing. She'd seen it on TV.

"I…" Lettie curled up in an armchair, tapping the sides. "No. Looked like we might for a minute, but in the end I fell asleep in his bed and he wandered off to one of the dead housemate rooms."

"Nice of him to spare you those, I suppose."

"Yeah. He's not all bad. So," she changed the topic with a lurch, clapping her hands, "did your bloke reply to you?"

"You mean Will?"

"Yeah. Took ages to get you to text him. Even longer to make you put kisses on the end."

"Thanks," Angelina sighed. "And no, he didn't, I guess he must…"

Before she finished bemoaning her failure, the phone buzzed in her hand and a message slid through. She expected Hobson with her marching orders, but it was Will.

Lettie leaned so far out of her armchair, she was in danger of falling. Angelina took pity on her and read out the message.

"*'Hi Angelina, sounds good,'*" her voice trembled, "*'let me know where and when.'* No kisses though." Her eyes flicked up to meet Lettie's. "Is that good?"

She guffawed. "Pretty decent, yeah."

"Okay. Um." She looked down at herself, realising she'd have no time to wash, change or put any make-up on before she had to be in Peckham to both work and meet Will. If she hadn't been drunk-texting, she might've foreseen these problems. Fucking hell. Could she call in sick? "Guess I have a date then. I think it's a date, anyway." Eyes back up at Lettie. "Is it a date?"

"Maybe."

"Thanks."

The phone rang, and this time it was exactly who she expected.

Giving Lettie a senseless nod, she picked up.

"Hi, Hobson?"

"Yeah, morning Choi."

Hobson dropped into the streetside bench near the IGS and exhaled heavily. He'd marched with military vigour to get out of there before Jacq reached her desk. The stretch of alleyway between the building and the road had been the worst part. She could've entered the foyer in time to see him walking down it. Thanks to his greater-than-average height, he was easy to spot from a distance.

"How, um, did you do? Did you find a way out of doing the thing?" Choi said, not taking the silence well.

"I…" For a moment, he almost spat out the whole truth about last night, but stopped himself. "Didn't find much. You?"

"Um, Ric said he saw the tracksuit guys shoving packages of drugs down the throats of dogs."

"Fuckin' hell. These people love dogs. Or maybe really hate them." He hunched over on his bench. "Okay. So I guess I either do this drug run or just ditch the case."

"You could always ditch it," Choi said, to his slight surprise.

"No, I…" Everything Jacq said the previous night hit him like a blow to his hungover head, on top of Ellie and Choi's disdain during the Rush case. "No, I'll do it. I said I would. Feel bad for the Vole family if the prick gets knifed."

"Wow. Okay." Choi sounded a little stunned. She'd better be amazed at his moral character. "What can I do?"

"Just get to Peckham like we said. Make sure Operation Stinks-Of-Shit goes according to plan. Don't worry about me, Choi, I'll be fine."

"Can't you call Ellie? Get her to do you a favour?"

Hobson slammed his eyes shut. "No. Don't think so."

"Okay. Good luck, I guess."

"Thanks. You too. Bye."

As the call bleeped off, Hobson opened his eyes. Ellie's anger, Jacq's disappointment and even the wretched terror of enslaved accountant Greg James floated there, unbidden.

Still, nothing else to do now but get on with it. Hobson groaned his way off the bench and into the cold morning air.

SIXTEEN
WALKING THE DOG

"That's a big fucking dog."

The last time Hobson was so close to a hound that size, he nearly lost a leg. Not that he'd developed a phobia – those were bullshit – but he still backed up a step.

Unfortunately, the dog in question wouldn't let him get away so easily. It was huge, black and looked like it was smiling all the time. Its tongue lolled out, light streaks ran through its fur – not unlike the greying in Hobson's own hair – as it panted and stared up at him.

Joseph was sitting on the bench behind the dog, grinning at Hobson's obvious discomfort. His burnt head and scarred-up face contorted into a death-mask of schadenfreude.

"Yes, this is Markus. He is a good boy." Joseph patted the seat next to him. "Sit now."

Pulling his eyes away from the panting face, Hobson obeyed. They were on a picnic table out the back of The Left Hand at nine in the morning.

Usually the garden wouldn't yet be open, but as ever, Micro made special exceptions for gangster arseholes.

The spring sunshine warmed him too much already. This summer was going to be a blazer.

"So," Joseph began with relish. "You will be transporting coke, yes, but you may be surprised to hear *exactly how* you will be doing this. You see…"

"Oh, for fuck's sake." Hobson rubbed his temples. "It's in the fucking dog, I *know*. I'm a detective, I looked into it." He glanced down at said dog, who wuffed and started licking Hobson's boots.

"Ah, I see." Joseph fell into a sullen silence, reaching into his trouser pocket and handing Hobson a business card. *Pauline's Pizza* was scrawled across it in a terrible handwriting font. The hazy shape of a pizza floated behind the name, an address in Brixton Village at the bottom.

"You are leading Markus here," Joseph said, jabbing at the card for added clarity. "A woman will take him from you. You are calling when it's done. Okay?"

"Yeah." Hobson stared at the card. "All clear."

Emerging from Brixton tube, Hobson tripped over a range of grumpy commuters. The lingering remainder of rush hour stumbled around him, someone barked something savage about "what kind of moron brings a dog on the tube", but Hobson ignored him. For all that guy knew, he could be blind.

The main concourse was big enough for him to drag Markus away from the foot traffic through the middle, a current dragging everything in its path inexorably towards the ticket barriers. He tugged his furry charge across the entrance cavern, then together they tackled the off-white stairs. Thankfully the dog's legs were long enough to ascend easily, a few passers-by even stopped to admire him. Much better.

Hobson's good mood was only dented when he emerged onto the street, a wide open entrance that dominated the main road like some kind of temple. Other underground stations were just functional doorways to the tunnel below, but this one was an attention seeker.

It all felt too exposed, and that was before he spotted a few police weaving around the crowd. He tried not to let his eyes widen at their bright green vests, but still, not a great sight when smuggling contraband.

Hell, they stopped a guy on the adjoining paving slab and searched his backpack. Clearly authorities were cracking down – was that why Joseph crammed coke into dogs?

Speaking of which, Markus dashed around, drawing compliments from yet more strangers. A little girl rushed over to pat him on the nose, Markus wuffed and stood still so she could stroke his back, eyes closed with expectation. Considering the pooch must've been ill-treated for ages, Hobson didn't know where he got it from. The kid giggled until her mother called her back. She gave Hobson enough of a look to know it was the enormous man making her uncomfortable, rather than the dog.

He'd seen a sign pointing to Brixton Village, and after a few minutes strolling around the corner, he plunged into a dark-green covered maze of small businesses. Nail bars, cash exchange shops, strange-looking booze joints, overly trendy food outlets, small counters with electronics piled around them and a coffee shop which appeared to be modelled after a tree house. A mixed food smell assaulted his nose, echoing voices knocked into his ears. Hobson shouldered through the thin mist of shoppers, finding Markus required more and more dragging to keep moving.

The shopfronts themselves were mostly wood-effect. Prices high, salvaged splintered furniture, trendies everywhere. When catering to the hipsters, the more ramshackle your joint looks, the better. Might explain all the naked-wood tables, plain-coloured facades and tiny metallic buckets of chips.

As they passed more coffee and burger stalls, the dog scrabbled back the way they came with rising passion. Soon enough, Hobson felt the stares of passing flatcaps turn against him as he hauled the flailing animal along.

Markus's desperate tugs in the opposite direction almost forced him to stop. But then Hobson looked up at the latest delightful red wood-stained sign.

Pauline's Pizza.

Jackpot.

But he was nowhere near getting the dog over to it; Markus stretched his lead to the max and whined like a puppy. Hobson took another look inside the restaurant. The massive front window revealed six tables and a couple of skinny folk eating thin pizza in darkness. The toppings weren't any he recognised, one of them looked like someone's garden. An earnest-looking waitress rushed around. Not a big place, but still empty. Well, it was only eleven in the morning.

The middle-aged woman behind the counter turned away from the cash register to look over towards him. She was buttoned all the way up while everyone else wore white t-shirts, her eyes glazed and terrifying. Her hair was pulled back severely, a pizza wheel attached to her leg in a brown leather Wild West holster. Must be Pauline.

And it looked like she was his contact, as she lunged across her restaurant to get to him. However, at the same time, Markus's barking reached a screaming critical mass. He pedalled his paws on the floor so desperately, both he and Hobson nearly tripped up.

Pauline was at the door now, hand reaching for that pizza wheel.

Markus whined with terror.

Hobson turned back on himself and stormed away, Markus trotting behind him.

Funnily enough, the hound seemed much happier going in this direction.

Hobson quickstepped out from the covered market, shoving a few teenagers and old people to one side as he went. He didn't have much experience with dogs, but it felt like Markus did *not* want to go anywhere near Pauline's Pizza. Perhaps he was placing too much faith in natural canine senses, but there must be some awful reason.

After all the shitty outcomes he'd sat through recently, he might be willing to deliver some coke to a pizza place for a quiet life. Still, handing this harmless (if also brainless) creature over to suffer seemed a step too far. Not if there was a way around it.

He dived into a nearby corner shop and bought two cans of dog food, making sure to get tins with a ring-pull – Hobson did not carry a tin-opener.

While he was there, he also swiped four carrier bags.

Thus armed, he sat down on a bench near Brixton Village and pulled Markus up next to him.

"How's it going, dog?" He stroked the enormous furry head as it strained to pant at passers-by. "Not up for pizza?"

Markus wuffed.

"Mm." Hobson picked up one of the tins of food, then started working his huge finger through the ring-pull. He had no nails, so it required a great deal of swearing, but eventually the metal sheared away.

As the can ripped open, the fresh, raw smell rose up Hobson's nose and he crinkled his face. The dog, meanwhile, almost knocked him off the bench trying to get to the juicy meat. As Hobson suspected, they'd been starving Markus to stop him shitting the drugs out. Poor little bastard.

Not wanting the hungry idiot to cut his muzzle on the tin, Hobson emptied the contents onto a plastic bag stretched out on the seat next to him. Markus descended on the small pile with a ferocious, wet gobbling sound. Within a minute, he was licking remains off the blue surface. In that time, Hobson had the second can open and was emptying that out to go the same way.

Hobson looked around the street. The way everyone was glancing over, they thought he was a homeless guy with some poor, helpless dog. What came next wouldn't alleviate that assumption.

Come to think of it, seemed odd Joseph *hadn't* asked Hobson to pull the coke out of Markus' faeces himself. He couldn't express any surprise at all that it came to this in the end.

Even so, he recoiled on instinct ten minutes later, as the dog squeezed his turds out onto the Brixton pavement. Markus whined a little as he went, struggling to pass the yellow drug-filled condoms. The splashes of rubber only peeked through at a few lightly coated intervals in the streaks of brown. Looks from other pedestrians became less sympathetic.

Nonetheless, Hobson waited for everything to pass, then put a plastic bag over his hand and started scooping the whole mess up. He kept his eyes fixed on the bench, refusing to notice the texture.

Within a few minutes, shaking off the need to vomit from the smell, he'd scraped all the dogshit into a carrier bag. Brown smears only made it through to his skin in a couple of places.

Wiping himself down with another bag, Hobson stood up and made his way back into Brixton Village. From one hand, he dangled a cheap blue carrier of poo, the other wrapped around the dog's lead. Markus wasn't as terrified by Pauline's Pizza now, but still pulled away as they got nearby.

This time, Pauline saw them coming a mile off. She hurried outside, hair rock solid in that bun, and only registered a small growl of annoyance when she spotted the bag of shit in his hand.

"Ah, Ms Pauline, I presume," Hobson gave the most charming smile he could manage. "I'm here to give you this dogshit."

Her face did not enjoy that news. "I was under the impression you were here to give us *the dog*."

"Change of plan. Look," he said, determined not to sound like a beggar, "you'd have to root through the shit anyway. Far as I can see, I've done half the work for you."

He held out the bag, and she recoiled, refusing to reach out and take it. Maybe she usually employed people to do this part. Hobson shrugged and dropped the shit-bag on the floor just outside her restaurant. It squelched into a flatter blob, the plastic sticking to the turd within.

"Take it or leave it, Ms Pauline. Have a nice day."

He took one more look into her tiny, beady, unblinking eyes. Poor Markus stretched his lead to its greatest possible extension, then sat at the end. Every so often, he barked at passers-by, as if imploring them to save him.

She ground her teeth at him, hand tapping on her holstered pizza wheel, and Hobson refused to look away. If possible, he got an even more overt warning vibe from Pauline than Edward Lyne. At least Lyne was merely an immoral capitalist – this woman felt like she'd fuck Hobson up just for disobeying her.

Part of him wanted to wait and watch her peel up that splat in front of him, but best not press his luck. He was already disobeying orders.

Hobson turned and walked away, taking Markus with him. If Pauline wanted to pizza-wheel him in the back, she could get on with it. Still held his breath as he left though.

Only exhaled once they'd turned a corner away from her restaurant.

"So, Markus," he said to the gleeful dog as they emerged from Brixton Village. "Wanna meet my friend Choi? Peckham ain't far by bus, I reckon we got time before... well, I dunno, I suppose I have to take you back to the psychos up north? Don't I?"

"Wuff!" said Markus, not giving him any guidance at all.

SEVENTEEN
S.O.S.

"It fucking stinks out here, Angie."

Not how Angelina herself would phrase it, but hard to deny Lettie's point. There was an overpowering stench at Peckham Rye station that morning. She'd felt tingles in her nose as they descended from the high platforms, but the familiar, comforting fuel smell of trains masked the worst of it. Still, the beginnings of a bad feeling stirred, like remembering she'd left that milk in the fridge too long.

As they entered the main downstairs ticket hall, Violet gagged, red hair falling over her face as she jerked her neck forwards. Her blue jacket protected her from the cold but not the air itself. Angelina wrinkled up her nose. Melodrama would accomplish nothing, better to take shallow breaths and keep walking.

With a climactic bleep, Angelina passed the ticket barriers. One problem with Operation Stinks-Of-Shit (as Hobson charmingly called this case) – it made exiting the station harder. Outward-going commuters rammed their way in, desperate to get up the stairs and above the smell.

Angelina tried to skirt to the left, creep along the wall. Lettie choked and staggered along behind, lack of grace getting her bumped harder. Edging around the ticket machines, they reached the covered walkway separating the station from the road.

And there, spread all the way out like a farmer's field full of crops, was Operation S.O.S. So much rubbish, oozing and stinking, a rough path beaten through the middle by desperate men and women trying to get to work.

There was *so much* of it – did Hobson ask for this? Not just a few piles, but total carpeting. The sacks of bilge spanned far and wide, a black plastic sea. Stacked in rows up to the street, shining, glistening blobs oozing from splits in the bags.

Taking a step out into the field of filth, she saw brown rotted vegetable pulp spilling into her walkway. The contents of Angelina's stomach rose up to meet the goop outside. She lifted a hand to cover her mouth and ran headlong down the courtyard. Her feet smashed down, bodyweight leaning too far forward in her desperation, trying to angle herself away from the smell.

Local residents in suits and hipsterwear alike were scampering up towards the station entrance. At the far end, a collection of green high-vis vests picked at the rubbish, throwing it into a skip behind them. Even with masks over their faces, they kept gagging and turning away. Desperate to keep moving, Angelina threaded around them and out into the road. She gasped as the air finally freshened.

Moments later, Lettie Vole caught up with her, one sleeve clamped tight over her nose.

"So," she rasped, "did you do it? Is this a good enough shitty stench for your boss?"

"I'm not sure," Angelina said. "Kinda worried it might be *too* much."

The noxious vapour reached down into her soul. Angelina shut her mouth tight and walked as fast as she could up the road without breaking into a run, knees firm and brittle. Lettie, though, murmured "Ah, fuck this," and legged it. Angelina followed suit after a second.

They scampered up the street, cutting through a small crowd. Many gathered to stare at the masked guys clearing the entrance to the station, smartphones raised high to capture the best angle. Considering how many online photo apps splattered a yellow filter over everything, this meadow of stewing disgust would translate well. Maybe Angelina should've taken a pic herself from the station entrance for their official account – imagine the likes!

Past the crowd, down the road, not walking into any bags of rubbish for once, Angelina turned into Jamie's Café. Deserted, no early morning crowd, just two guys sitting at a table: The Pimp and Bible-Amp Benny, as they'd agreed. Lettie bundled in behind her and looked around.

"So, what're we doing here?"

She also spoke far too loud, considering only their two clients and proprietor Jamie were in the room.

"We're just checking in," Angelina said, awkward as everyone listened. Even with Lettie to keep her company, she didn't enjoy this.

"Glad to hear it, young lady," said The Pimp, staring at Lettie instead of her for once. "You did a good job."

"You reckon?" Angelina kept her voice level. "Thanks, I guess."

"Why are you wearing that hat?" Lettie gestured at the huge red velvety top hat which he was, indeed, still sporting. "I mean, how'd you even get through the door?"

"I took it off. I don't think we've had the pleasure, miss…?"

"Touch me and I'll kill you." Lettie turned the death glare on him and he laughed. Angelina didn't crack so much as a smirk.

Instead, she turned to Benny, looking smooth in his estate agent suit. Clearly not even bothering with his preaching today, thanks to the sheer scale of their achievement. "You okay?" Angelina said. "Is this helping?"

"All is well," Benny replied, giving her a big grin. "I appreciate your strivings. If nothing else, you've certainly achieved the promised plague."

"You seem very, um, calm about it all."

"Well, what is there to get upset about? It's not every day someone does this in my name. It's positively biblical." Benny leaned back in his chair with a warm smile, before catapulting himself to his feet in a sudden jerk. "But now, ladies, I must to work. Keep me posted, won't you?"

"Absolutely. C'mon, Lettie," Angelina nodded to the clients, pulling her friend away before The Pimp could say anything. "Let's check in with Jamie."

Of course, Jamie's Café was so cramped, the excuse didn't carry them far. They scrambled across the room, still delighted to get away even if only a few metres.

Then she reached Jamie's counter, smile in place ready for her big heroine's welcome, only to find the apron-clad owner staring down at them impassively.

"Morning, Jamie."

"Angelina. And who's your friend? She seems less difficult than the last one."

"This is Lettie, she's okay. So, how did you find everything? I saw there was loads of rubbish left out?"

"I gotta say, I was a tad disappointed."

"How?"

"Well," he indicated his empty café, "no customers. Everyone is either hiding from the smell or watching the clean-up. I didn't anticipate how successful you'd be at destroying the neighbourhood."

Nobody walked by outside. The jug by Jamie's milk-frother sat untouched.

"Yeah, I'm kinda surprised by that myself," Angelina murmured.

"And what's your plan to deal with it?"

"Maybe... less rubbish tomorrow?" she ventured.

"So you don't have a long-term strategy at all?"

"Look," Lettie cut in, "Hobson is busy with something more important right now, okay?" Angelina had trouble keeping her groan inside. "But he'll be here soon and then we'll work on getting your little shop going again."

After that, she couldn't drag Lettie away fast enough, as a cold fury rose in Jamie's eyes. Shame, he seemed decent, not to mention also being right: they needed to work out where to go with this. Hopefully Hobson would have a roadmap in mind, once he finished distributing drugs and turned up.

To avoid recognition or arrest, the two of them fled the high street. After a roundabout, mostly silent walk, they ended up next to a row of windy bus shelters, near a huge supermarket. Hobson would arrive any moment to take charge, and in the meantime, Angelina tried to manage her personal business.

"Hey, Will, still on for lunchtime? How about..." She composed out-loud. It was nearly midday, not much time before their proposed lunch date and if she didn't text soon, he might make other plans.

If only she had a clue where was trendy. Didn't want to chance a pub on their first date, she was too damn underage.

"Hey, Lettie," she tried, "would you judge someone if they took you to Subway for lunch?"

"Subway? Bit shit, but could be worse. Can always sit somewhere else and eat it. And at least you can always top that on the next date."

"Mm." Angelina stood back against the wall as another few kids shoved past, staring at their phones. Lettie shoulder-barged one of them, giving Angelina a blood pressure spike. They just walked on.

An engine roared behind them as the 345 bus pulled in. Angelina hammered out the rest of the message and sent it; she might not get another chance. Subway would have to do for a first effort. Shame she wasn't dating Hobson, except *yuck*.

Speaking of her boss, he stomped off the bus accompanied by a large, friendly looking dog, a dark skipping thing with light streaks in his fur. Unexpected.

"Hi." Angelina waved, cautious. "Is that dog full of drugs?"

"No, he's dumped them out now. This is Markus, girls. Markus, this is Lettie and Choi. They're both okay when you get to know them."

"Wuff!" said Markus. He had a big, happy face and was now smacking at Lettie's trainers with a paw. Angelina wasn't a cute animal fan, but this was a hard creature to hate.

But Violet Vole refused to be distracted by the adorability of Markus.

"So, wait, you took this dog from the gangsters?" Her eyes narrowed, face turning an angrier shade of red. "Angie said you were meant to hand it over. What the *fuck* does this mean for my *shitting brother?*"

If Hobson had a ready answer, Angelina knew he'd spit it right into Lettie's face.

Complete silence fell.

But it wasn't all bad news: Angelina's phone vibrated, delivering a reply from Will saying Subway sounded *lovely*.

"Look, your shitting brother will be *fine*, we just need to... I mean, look at him," Hobson said, indicating Markus's fluffy face. "He doesn't understand all this, he's clearly got no brain. I got the drugs out of him, there's no need for him to go back to the Makozmo Centre For Canine Narcotic Bum-Filling."

"Wuff!" said Markus, licking mud off Lettie's shoe.

"Oh, for fuck's sake." The increasingly scarlet Vole scowled, inhaled with deep scorn and turned away. "Do you even have a real plan? Why didn't you just hand over the dogs like they wanted you to?"

"Let's get away from this bus stop for Christ's sake," Hobson pointed towards the nearest looming shop, imagining the high street lurking beyond. "Away we go."

Lettie turned in the instructed direction, but couldn't relax for a second. "You are at least going to give him back to them if they ask, aren't you?"

His ignoring the question didn't seem to cheer her up.

Hobson tugged on Markus' lead and off they all went, around the edge of the bus terminal. Lettie marched ahead, determined not to let anyone get in the way of her strop.

"I have to say," Choi began, "I didn't take you as the type to lose it over a cute doggy."

"It's just…" Hobson looked down at Markus, back at Choi and at the heavens. "Can't we draw some kind of line? Do we have to shit on everyone? You're the one who wanted to stop helping slave-drivers or whatever."

"It's only a dog, Hobson."

"Yeah? I thought you teenagers loved the fuckin' fluffy-wuffy animal-wanimals."

"Apparently I'm not like the others." Choi looked down at the dog in question and stopped for a few seconds, knelt down and rubbed the back of his head. Markus leaned his neck into her hand. "Although he does seem nice."

"Wuff!" said Markus.

"Exactly," Hobson smiled.

"Yeah." Choi got up and carried on. "Still think you're being stupid though."

Lettie showed no interest in stopping for man or beast. The other three trailed in her wake, around the outside of the supermarket, through a small shopping arcade and down the road. They skirted a few more people on the street, until they were back by Jamie's Café.

Outside, staggered up and down the street, were a group of men and women in bright green vests. Their other most prominent features were big hair and clipboards. The old charity fundraising team, chased down the road.

"Ah," Hobson said, "I see we got them away from the station. Benny must be pleased?"

"Um, yeah, he's alright," Choi muttered. "Though Jamie was a bit annoyed about us driving customers from his café by stinking the street out."

"Well, not as if we work round the corner anymore, is it?" Hobson said, smile not diminishing. "I'll have a chat with him, it'll be piss-easy. He can pet my new dog."

But no sooner had he turned toward the café doorway, Jamie appeared in the way. His brows frowned so low, they almost covered his eyes.

"What?" Lettie snarled. "Let us in. We'll buy coffees."

"No, sorry," Jamie shook his head. "Enough of you people."

Hobson moved to the front. "Problem?"

"You wrecked the station and now no-one will come near my café because these people with clipboards are in front of it!" He gestured at the array of chuggers. Down the road, mysterious masked men were emptying rubbish out of the station entrance. "Enough of you."

"C'mon, mate, it's just…"

"Oh, shove it up your arse, *mate*. And you can't bring that thing in here either."

"You mean Markus? But he's so fucking friendly."

"I mean it, Hobson. Away with you. Should never have helped with your idiotic plan in the first place."

Jamie disappeared into his café, and Hobson turned to the other two. Choi stared as if someone knocked her over the head, while Lettie planted her hands on her hips. No-one had anything useful to contribute.

"What the hell happened here, Choi?" he said, at last.

"Think we may have overkilled the rubbish-dumping somehow. I spoke to all the shop owners down here and they said they left a bag or two out but dunno where the huge mass of shite came from."

"Okay," he said. "Spoken to Will yet?"

"No," she muttered.

"Well, let's do that now then."

Choi's face dropped even further, Lettie roared out the beginning of another *"What about my brother?"*

Hobson waved them both off and led the whole convoy down the street. Even though he was still taking regular painkillers for his leg, the two of them were giving him a headache.

Will's reply text to Angelina suggested meeting around one o'clock at the local Subway. It was twenty to that hour now, and she was entering his reception area. Even worse, she was accompanied by Hobson and an agitated Lettie, not to mention a large, dopey dog.

When they first entered, Will was smooth and calm as ever, but his eyes widened when he saw Markus. "Okay, um, guys, I'm cool, but that dog isn't going to make a mess is he?"

"Markus? No, he's fine. Say hello to Will, dog."

"Wuff!" said Markus, before approaching a tall decorative plastic houseplant and trying to eat it. Hobson yanked him away after the first mouthful.

"Right. Good." Rubbing his temples, Will turned to her. "Angelina, hi. You alright?"

"I'm good, thanks." Should she mention looking forward to their lunch later? "You?"

"I'm alright, I'm alright. How can I help you guys?"

"Wondered if you could give us any clue what the fuck's happening here with this station-dumping plan? Choi says the shopkeepers put a bag or two each out, so we're not quite sure how shit got so fucked? I'm not going anywhere near the place, but she says it's like a gas attack out there."

"Oh, yeah," Will said, looking sheepish, "sorry, I might've overdone it a bit. Got some friends round, we moved pretty much all the week's trash from the whole Brightman."

"What?" Hobson burst out laughing. "Why?"

He shrugged. "You… you both… I dunno. You guys wanted help."

Angelina felt her mouth hanging open and clipped it shut. She wasn't sure if that was sweet or stupid. Or maybe he was just sucking up to Hobson. Perhaps she had no idea what was going on.

"Okay. Jesus. Fucking kids." Hobson definitely gave Angelina an exasperated look as he said that. "Don't do shit tomorrow, alright? We'll need to re-assess this. Sadly, bigger fish to fry first."

He looked over at Lettie, who'd given in and started petting the dog. "Lettie. We need to deal with Pete, ideally without getting Markus taken back to the ketamine kennels. Can you get me a chat with him?"

"With my brother?"

"Yes."

She gulped. "You're not going to hurt him are you?"

"Not as much as these twats with knives would."

"Fine. I'll call them now and see if we can visit."

"Thanks. As soon as possible, please."

Hobson exhaled as Lettie scurried away, placated for now. Angelina sidled over. "Do I have time to go for lunch here before we head off?"

"No. We gotta get moving. Work to do."

She looked over at Will, who shrugged and smiled gently. He didn't look *devastated* exactly, but maybe she saw a little disappointment in his eyes.

EIGHTEEN
INTERVIEW WITH THE WOLF-MAN

Mid-afternoon in the police station nearest Markham Road. The sun was still there outside, Hobson remembered, but it didn't reach down to the cells. On the other side of a desk, guarding the entrance, there was a policeman.

"Evening, sarge." Hobson contorted his face into a sincere smile. He didn't usually give a shit about police who weren't Ellie, but now she'd cut him off the favours list, time to give arse-kissing a shot. "How's it going?"

The policechap in question was tall and skinny all over, including the face, a tall yet wavering column. His arms moved like a crane, pivoting around the elbow-joint.

Despite Hobson's efforts at making friends, the uniformed pole didn't even bother addressing him. Instead, he turned straight to Violet Vole.

"Miss Vole, you said you and some others wanted to visit your brother, you didn't mention it was *him*."

"Sorry," said Hobson, determined to stay happy. "Do we know each other?"

"We met at a party when you were still with Ellie. You told me I was probably a tree."

"Oh. Sorry. Imagine I was quite drunk."

"Yes." The creaky tree-man looked down at his paperwork. Was he talking so slowly to punish them, or did his wooden brain struggle to transmit thoughts?

"So," said Lettie, "*can* we see him?"

The policeman tapped his pen on the desk, in a rhythm that could lull babies to sleep. "I suppose so. But not for long. Is she going in as well?"

A skinny index twig pointed at Choi.

"Yes," said Hobson, before anyone could say otherwise. "She's a relative. Very close. Very sad."

"Right," said the policeman, shaking his head. "Close cousin, I suppose. Enfield by way of Taiwan."

Hobson checked if Choi was offended, but her face registered nothing. Also occurred to him he'd no idea *where* her roots were either — somewhere Asia-ish? Was he racist for not asking? He filed it away for later. Despite the ethnic uncertainty, the visit seemed to be going ahead — perhaps Ellie still watched over him.

The admin cop continued. "You can't take that dog into an interview room, by the way."

"Wuff," said Markus, sounding sad.

"Okay," Hobson nodded, "but it's cool if I leave him out here, yeah? I can tie him to the radiator?"

The police guy nodded, made one last slow, looping stroke with his biro. He stood up, lurching in slow motion around his desk and opened up the door into the dark. Despite himself, Hobson felt a gulp of fear.

The three of them sat on stiff, uncomfortable chairs in some kind of interview room, waiting. Angelina stared at the ceiling, the walls, the floor – anything, in short, except her fellow visitors. Some police architect had honed this room to careful blandness: blue, white and reinforced window. No posters or decoration, nothing to see except occasional stains or marks.

The door swung open, scraping unpleasantly along the floor, and the lanky policeman entered, followed by a bowed figure in a beige nothing-suit. Behind them stomped a more conventionally scary musclecop.

The man in the middle, of course, was Pete Vole. His red hair was filthy, face vacant. The pointed, manic face seemed even scarier as the skin pulled tight around it. She supposed being locked up and threatened would do that to a person.

He tumbled into the seat opposite them, across the cheap metal table. Once comfortable, his eyes flicked up just high enough to make contact. Even the sight of his sister didn't get much reaction.

"Hello, Mister Hobson," Pete said, "what do you want?"

The question went ignored for the moment. The two police, tall one and lumpy one, had retreated to the entrance, but stayed on this side of it. Hobson turned to them. "You two, any chance of some fuckin' privacy?"

"Nope, sorry," the first cop said. "You're not his lawyer, you're not entitled to it. Think yourself lucky you're in here at all. Especially with *her*."

A spindly finger jabbed at Angelina and she sank in her seat.

"Right." Hobson looked back at Pete. "Mister

Vole, we hear you've been having security problems, even *with* the valiant efforts of London's Finest twatting around near your cell."

"Yup," Pete jerked before he spoke, as if his spirit was booting back up. "I don't understand it. Took two failed stabbings by the same guy before he got moved away. It's as if they don't care for my human rights."

"Imagine," Hobson said, shaking his head. "Imagine that."

"And all this," Pete continued, volume climbing, "just in a holding cell at some police station. I don't know how they expect me to manage in a real prison, what with all these pricks out to get me. But I'm not worried, Mister Hobson, I'm *not*, because I know they've got redundancy after redundancy in place to protect me." His eyes huge with mania, he flat-out yelled at the cops: *"Isn't that right, guys?"*

"Hey," said the larger of the policemen, staying impressively calm, "even other prisoners don't like crazy serial killers. What did you expect? A surprise party?"

Lettie hissed out a sigh and entered the conversation, punching Hobson on the shoulder harder than necessary. "For fuck's sake. Enough. You're not here to help him aggravate the police. Either find out something useful or give up your fucking dog."

Pete chuckled and raised a curious eyebrow. "You've got a dog too? Is it like my old one?"

"Markus is *nothing like that*, you little shit," Hobson snapped.

"Come on," Angelina butted in. "We just need to know if you have any ideas about what they *want*. Like, did they make any demands when they attacked you?"

"Sorry, sweetie," Pete gave her a too-wide grin, Angelina felt her forehead warm up. "Just big men lunging at me with jagged stuff. Barely survived this morning."

"This morning?" Hobson leaned in. "The guy came at you *this* morning?"

"Yeah. Spilled my porridge."

"Fuck." His eyes narrowed. "Fuck."

"What?" Lettie said.

"This morning," Angelina murmured, "Hobson was... you know, *negotiating* with them this morning. Which means they should have stopped trying to kill Pete until he'd finished."

"Which means they're going to fucking kill him anyway." Hobson finished her sentence. "Which means it doesn't matter if we give Markus back."

"You..." Lettie slammed a fist down on the table, then snatched it away in obvious pain. "You can't just not... it's his only chance!"

"He's got no chance." Hobson turned back to the two policemen. "Oi, lawmen. This cunt is in serious danger. Put him in solitary or whatever, keep everyone else away, and if you don't and he dies, I'll get my intern to put it on Twitter. Clear?"

"Come on, Hobson," the tall constable said, still talking like a stroke victim. "We can't be expected to give people special treatment every time a fight breaks out."

"Also, I'll tell Detective Sergeant Ellie and she'll fuck you up. Any questions?"

They shut up and scowled.

"Well, Pete," Hobson got up. "Imagine you're about to get moved to real prison if they can't protect you here. I'd say I'm sorry, but I'm not."

"It's fair enough, Mister Hobson." He smiled and practically danced in his seat. "I don't know why you're helping at all, considering I killed her boyfriend."

He gestured towards his sister.

Hobson was struck quiet by that, and fair enough – so was Angelina. Both looked at Lettie.

Violet glowered down at her brother. Worked her way out of her seat to upright, sucked her lips in and spat across the table at him. It spattered across his forehead and nose.

"Matt was worth ten of you, you dickhead, but Mum would be heartbroken if you died. This is the last time I waste my fucking time visiting." She turned to Hobson. "Are we finished?"

"Yeah."

So the police moved to take him away. Didn't give him anything to wipe the phlegm off his face, and fair enough.

"Mister Hobson," Joseph's voice spat from the mobile phone into his ear, "I hear you went on the walkabouts with our dog. When I ask you to do a straightforward task, you are better served to just be fucking doing it. That dog is trained and used to our routine. If it isn't back with us in The Left Hand by end of day, Pete Vole won't be the only sorry one."

He clicked off without saying goodbye, and Hobson turned to the others, moving his neck as slow as he could. In yet another bus shelter near the police station, the two women sat in a row. Their eyes were wide, saucer-like and lasering into his.

"So, guys," Hobson said at last, "seems Joseph and his mates do want the dog back quite angrily."

"So that's enough shitting around and you'll be

taking it back?" Lettie hissed.

"I…" Hobson dropped eye contact for a second, teeth clenching at the thought of Joseph's sneering tone. "I think I'm gonna head over to The Left Hand, take another stab at negotiating. You guys keep Markus for safekeeping…"

"For Christ's sake," she roared, "just give them back the dog. There's no way they'll listen if you don't. Much more of this shit and they'll be after *us*, never mind Pete."

"Right." He turned to the other onlooker. "Choi, casting vote: what do you think we do?"

"Well," she began, taking a nervous glance either way, "I don't know if we should give him back *right* away. Hobson's right, they want to kill Pete anyway. You want some kind of assurance."

"Oh, he's just using this as an excuse," Lettie snapped. "He was always gonna pull this shit, because he wants to feel like a big man or a hero or whatever."

"Good, Choi." Hobson grinned, blanking Lettie totally. "That means you win custody of the dog *and* the angry Vole sister. Enjoy."

He threw Choi the lead. "Keep an eye on Lettie and don't do anything stupid. Hopefully I'll be back in a few hours. Y'know, if they don't kill me."

"Wait," Choi called out before he got far away. "Where do we go?"

"Back to the office, I suppose." He took one more step, then turned back again. "If Jacq says anything weird about me, just ignore it."

NINETEEN
LIFE CHOICES

"So, you didn't get your date with Will, huh?" Lettie gave a sympathetic smile.

"No, I guess not. But he still seemed happy to see me, didn't he?"

Angelina's last question went unanswered as they approached the Inspiration Gestation Station. Needy silence descended like a dark cloud.

"Yeah," said Lettie, at last.

Violet Vole kept complaining about Hobson's *attitude, obsession with this dog* and *fucking refusal to prioritise her family* all the way back. Eventually, annoyed by Angelina's stubborn siding with her boss, she started texting instead.

Seeing Pete again reminded Angelina of his smug, unsettling creepiness. She looked down at the dog trotting along with them, short tail swishing and streaks in his fur standing out against the night. Angelina knelt down to stroke him. If she could save only one out of Markus or Pete from a fire, might have to rule against Lettie's brother.

They reached the glass front door of the building, light still glowed in reception. Angelina had no key card, but whenever she approached the building, Jacq would open up.

And there she was, sitting at her desk. Angelina reached up to knock on the glass. As Markus barked at the sound, she saw another figure at the desk, standing among the painted flowers. Curt blonde bob, nice suit – Emily Allen. The one Social Awesomer she hadn't seen since the Pete Vole case wrapped up.

The receptionist herself looked over and spotted them, but without the achingly sincere grin Angelina expected. Still, she discontinued her personal conversation to trot over and open the door. Her walk was lethargic, feet hardly leaving the floor.

Much like Will back in Peckham, she double-took when the dog pattered in. As soon as he entered reception, Markus stopped dead. He patted the astroturf with one paw, uncertain whether it was grass or carpet.

After a few exploratory pokes, Markus rolled over in the fake pasture, growled at it, then lay down. Angelina laughed, Jacq managed a soft *awww* noise.

"So, um, is he yours?" Jacq said, not looking away from the dog.

"Hobson's looking after him for someone," Angelina said, trying to sound authoritative. "And now I'm looking after him for Hobson."

She readied herself for Lettie's snide comment about why Hobson was *really* keeping the dog, but no joy.

"Hi Emily," Angelina added.

"Angelina," Emily said, with a thin smile. "How're things?"

"Oh, you know, busy. We're just going to take Markus upstairs until Hobson gets back."

"When's he coming back?" Jacq asked, voice squeaking.

"Oh, later," Angelina shrugged. "We'll just go upstairs, didn't mean to interrupt you guys."

She pulled on Markus' lead and he flailed himself upright. They hurried towards the lift.

"Might come up to the office with you, if that's okay," Emily called over as Angelina pressed the button. "Still got some stuff there, didn't want to let myself in. I gather Lettie went up alone yesterday and Hobson disapproved."

Emily bustled into the lift before Angelina could protest.

Hobson crossed the threshold of The Left Hand, feeling himself sweat as the weightless door drifted back into its frame. He was familiar with returning to a boss after a job, but coming empty-handed made his back slump.

Immediately, he noticed a lack of the muttering old men and pissed youngsters who usually populated McHellerman pubs. A few remained around the front towards the door, but as Hobson took his next steps inside, another couple gave up and headed for the exit.

The rest of the tables grew out of the back area, past the bar and spreading towards him into the light. The bald guys in shiny, easy-clean tracksuits and cheap t-shirts crowded around the front tables. They nursed their beers without taking a sip. All staring at him. Usually they stayed back, but this time the public up front were driven out. The illusion of normality was in tatters.

"Mister Hobson," Joseph said, looking around from a stool at the bar. His mouth pulled tight at one side thanks to that scar, turning his smile into a half-formed grimace. The stubbly mess on his head bounced the lighting in all directions.

"Joseph," Hobson said, hoping he wasn't showing fear. "How's it going?"

"That depends. Where might our fucking dog be?"

"Ah," Emily said as they returned to the old Social Awesome office, Markus rushing ahead. "I see you haven't changed the old place much. Except putting all our property into that pile."

Emily topped off her standard tidy suit and impeccable haircut with subtle but perfect make-up and an expertly enunciated British accent which couldn't be real. She came across like a teacher or disapproving aunt. Everything that seemed sensible to Angelina now felt like childish idiocy. She got enough of this shit from the mother she already had.

"Well, y'know, we've not been here long," Angelina mumbled. Markus rushed into the office and sniffed everything. He especially enjoyed the area where Matt Michaelson's arm was bitten off last week – must be interesting scents lingering.

"I'm sure they'll start making it their own soon," Lettie said, calmer and less enraged for some reason.

"Totally," Angelina agreed. "What did you say you wanted?"

"Oh, I just need to find something in Mister Lyne's old room."

"That's Hobson's office now, I'm not sure you should…" But Emily already invited herself into the side area, clicking the door open in spite of Angelina's valid protests.

Still, the work experience kid tried her best to supervise. Hobson seemed attached to the old Edward Lyne paperwork he was always rifling through, best stop Emily from stealing any. Angelina went over and lingered in the doorway, while the unwanted guest poked and prodded the pen-holder on Hobson's desk.

The silence settling over them was torturous. Probably why Emily said: "So, how are you finding your work experience?"

"Oh, y'know, it's exciting – scary but exciting. Last day tomorrow, think I'm doing okay."

"That's good," Emily said, not looking up.

"I mean, I worry I'm doing the wrong thing sometimes. But if I've learnt one thing from working here, it's that adults have the same problem. I mean, Hobson is totally freaked out right now and he's *old*."

"So *do* you think Hobson is doing the right thing at the moment?"

"Well, I mean… I think…" Was it just her, or was that a weird question to ask? Almost as if Emily knew about…

Angelina whipped around. The office was completely empty – Lettie gone, Markus too. Just as she processed this, she heard the lift roaring. The corridor outside remained deserted, so they must be in that capsule, surging downwards.

Her face tight with panic, she looked back to Emily. "You were just distracting me? You and Lettie planned this?"

Emily gave a small shrug, but didn't look sorry. "The two of you were just being stupid, Angelina. I'm sorry, but no matter what Pete did, he's a person and that's a dog, so..."

"Oh... *fuck you*," Angelina hissed, before turning and running to the stairwell door. Good job she hadn't taken her coat off yet.

"Well, the thing is, chaps," Hobson said. "I'm afraid there's a bit of a change of plan with regard to this whole dog business."

The angry crime men seemed underjoyed. Joseph, in particular, put his pint down with a pointed clunk before slipping off his stool. Slamming glasses echoed up and down the pub, as the henchmen followed his example. Hobson heard the last couple of regular punters slip out of the front door behind him. Couldn't blame them, really. Must be nice to have the option.

His fingers flicked. Joseph stood opposite him, arms crossed. "What are you meaning by that, Hobson?"

"*Mister* Hobson. And I am not in a fucking position to return your dog. Sorry about that."

"What position *are* you in, *Mister* Hobson?"

"Can't we come to some arrangement here? You scratch my back, I fix your bathroom, that kinda shit?"

"Fuck you and fuck your hot water pipe," Joseph hissed. His mouth twisted, scarred cheek stretching until Hobson thought it might tear open. "You think your shitty plumbing talk will work just because of where we are from? Patronising turd. Give us our dog or we kill Peter Vole *and* his little sister too."

Hobson's phone buzzed in his pocket, but they'd have to wait.

"Look, can we really not make a deal? How much money do you want? How about I just fuckin' pay you off?"

"Money?"

"Yeah," Hobson said, "how much to forget about Markus *and* Pete Vole?"

"To lose a trained dog *and* ignore a major insult?" Joseph looked around the room, trading grins with his goons. "Fifty thousand pounds."

"How many fucking pints have you *had?*" Hobson tried his best not to yell. "I could barely afford that if I sold my business and my intern."

"Then you will be giving us back our dog?"

"No. Well. Maybe. I don't know."

Hobson breathed in, broke eye contact at last and made for the bar. The usual barman was still there – so terrified by everyone else in the room, he didn't even give Hobson any attitude.

"Okay barkeep," Hobson said, with a sad smile, "two pints of that pale ale, please. One for me, the other for me ten minutes later."

TWENTY
BAD DECISIONS

Chasing someone down through the dark streets of London with everything at stake!

Yes, this was one experience Angelina half-hoped for when she started working at a detective agency. But much like all the others, second thoughts hit hard once it was really happening.

She thudded down Dalston looking for a hurrying redhead with a large dog, leapt around cats, bicycles and a million-and-one slow-walking people. It was getting dark. She kept almost running into pedestrians, dashing around children and trying to see over the road past swarms of buses.

Angelina didn't like this at all. Hobson wouldn't answer her phone calls, and now she was almost at the tube. No choice but to dive in and hope everything worked out.

As advertised, Hobson finished his first pint after ten minutes and started work on the second. He'd take this a bit slower.

Joseph remounted the stool next to him and gave conspicuous sideways eyeball. Hobson wouldn't be hurried, though. No idea what to do or say next, so time to regroup. He checked his phone – missed calls from Choi. Hopefully nothing disastrous.

All around him, a conspicuous sound of breathing, so loud he wondered if someone had a cold. Maybe this crowd had sat motionless so long, their respiration synchronised.

It was like being in the fucking Colosseum. Endless heavies, waiting for Hobson and Joseph to negotiate the living shit out of each other.

"So, what's going on, exactly? I mean," he said, as Joseph's stare moved closer, "you attacked Pete Vole while I was still doing your stupid errand. Why should I hand you back your fucking dog if you're going to kill Vole anyway?"

Joseph twitched hard, mouth opening and closing, dropping eye contact at last. His gaze was mobile, flicking side to side. The huge audience seemed to intimidate him, rather than empower him.

"Some people among us," he hissed, pointlessly, "were close to Yam Makozmo, and are not being convinced that anything is a substitute for Pete Vole's death. Rest assured, return the dog to show you have some respect and I will work on them until they are submitting."

Hobson nodded. "Well, *my* people would like proper assurances Pete Vole will be kept alive, so…"

"Just give us the dog, then!" Joseph's voice didn't scream, but sharpened. "It is just some animal, Mister Hobson, and I don't see why it matters so much to you."

"You gotta draw the line somewhere, Joseph. I've chosen Markus. Sorry for the fuckin' inconvenience."

RUSH JOBS

The breathing in the room fell out of sync. Hobson heard some of the muscle whispering among themselves while their leader was talking.

"Let me be clear, Mister Hobson," Joseph said, levelling his voice again. "You cannot talk around this point anymore. If you can't pay our price and won't give us the dog back, we kill both the Voles, maybe you as well. There are no back doors here for you. Are you saying that this is your final answer?"

"I..." Hobson felt like he was walking into a wall. "I suppose if there's no other..."

Since the doors to The Left Hand sat stationary for so long, Hobson assumed someone must have locked them. A bright red woman in a faded blue jacket burst through. She dragged a large, black-and-white dog with one hand, both of them gasping and wheezing louder than anyone else here. Lettie and Markus.

"What is this shit?" Joseph snapped. Hobson couldn't add much to that.

A slim, short figure in black and purple smashed through the door before it fell closed, rugby tackling herself into Lettie's midriff. Both of them crashed to the floor, knocking over a table and sending beer everywhere. Lettie lost her grip on Markus, so he trotted off to start licking it up.

"Choi, what the fuck?" Hobson groaned. Joseph wasn't the only one losing control of his associates. To give her credit, Choi managed a few ineffectual punches at Lettie's face before the bald swarm pulled them apart.

"So," Joseph said, "shall I be taking the dog or just killing Miss Vole? Since they are both helpfully being right here."

"Wuff!" said Markus.

"Hobson," Angelina huffed out, "sorry about this."

"Choi," he said, not hiding his disappointment. "What the fuck? You had one job."

"I..." She panted, only able to form a few syllables. Couldn't Hobson see she was dying? "I'm sorry. I know."

"Enough." Joseph, with his crusty disfigurements, was as horrid as she remembered. "Promise you'll drop this *now* or both Voles die. You are making a decision, Mister Hobson."

"For Christ's sake," Lettie called out, "I brought you the fucking dog, just take it and leave us alone."

Angelina stared at Hobson, waiting for him to say something. Would've held her breath, if her wrecked athletic agony didn't make that impossible.

Hobson rose from his bar stool, draining the remaining third of his pint. Looked at Markus, curled up next to Angelina's feet. The big detective's teeth gritted, eyes turning red.

He went over to Lettie, leaned in to talk to her. Angelina was close enough to overhear.

"For fuck's sake," he growled, "you couldn't leave alone, could you?"

"I'm very fucking sorry you're getting old and sentimental, Hobson," she snipped back. "But someone has to deal with shit. You're going to let my brother die? And didn't he just say he was going to kill me as well? What was I *meant* to do?"

"I wasn't going to let either of you idiots get stabbed. I just thought there might be another way which wasn't awful, just for once. But no, couldn't have that could we?"

"Oh, you were going to save the day like a big brave hero?"

"Piss off," Hobson scowled. Angelina thought he might punch her for a second.

"Like you've ever done anything like that," Lettie carried on. "You think you're some living legend, but Angie said the café dude in Peckham didn't even know who the fuck you are."

"I…" Something in Hobson's eyes flashed, but he didn't say anything else. Angelina gave Lettie the most betrayed scowl she could manage.

Hobson knelt down next to Markus and stroked him on the head. A half smile formed on his face as the dog leaned back into it,

Angelina waited for him to speak, but still nothing. Markus wuffed contentedly, until Hobson looked up at Joseph.

"You really won't just fuck off?"

"No. Not now." Joseph's scar tightened. "Have a reputation to be thinking of. Need to hear you say it."

"Of course you do."

The resigned sadness in Hobson's voice broke Angelina's heart. She took another furious peer at Lettie, who she blamed for this, no matter what anyone said.

Lettie shrugged back at her, as much arm movement as she could manage through the big dude holding her. The one behind Angelina let her go a while back. Probably didn't think the slight kid would be much threat, since she could barely lift a limb.

She kept giving Lettie the evils, but all she got in return was another shrug and a mouthed *'What else was I meant to do?'*

The awful part: Angelina didn't know.

Joseph, meanwhile, *wouldn't* fuck off. "So, we take the dog, yes Hobson, and you won't make a fuss? Since you can't give us the money or let us kill the Voles?"

Hobson stood back up straight. "I suppose so."

Angelina gave Lettie one last furious narrow look.

"Wait." Lettie's caustic voice shuddered out across the pub. "Money. How much money?"

Joseph jerked towards her. "What?"

"You said Hobson wouldn't give you the money to leave it be. Is there an amount you'll take to just go away?"

"I... Well," Joseph stammered again, before pulling his voice together. "I said I'd be dropping the whole affair for fifty thousand of pounds."

"Alright." Lettie looked back at Angelina with a chastened fury, then at Hobson. He seemed unsure what was going on.

"My family are pretty well-off. If I tell them you're threatening to kill both their kids and there's no other option, they'll find a way to pay. *Then* will you *please* just fuck the fuck off?"

"I suppose so, I..." He moved over to get in her face. "You *will* be dying if the money does not come through, do you understand?"

Lettie wrenched her shoulders away from the guy holding her and came forward to meet him. "Yes. I do. Now, do we have a deal? No stabbing any of us or Pete, and Hobson keeps the fucking dog?"

She stuck her arm out for the handshake. Joseph's eyes rolled either way, as if trying to gauge the mood of the crowd. At last, he reached out and shook on it. The room exhaled.

"Okay," Hobson said, "let's get the fuck out of here before they ask us to play a drinking game."

He picked up Markus' lead and went straight for the door, the other two quickstepping behind him. Angelina could feel Joseph's eyes on them, so she forced herself to move faster, even though her legs ached when she walked.

They stepped away from the pub, the cold air felt amazing on her stress-dampened skin. No-one spoke or paused until they reached the top of the road. Then Hobson turned back towards The Left Hand, still not quite looking at Lettie.

"Thanks," he said. "Appreciate it."

"Yeah," she said with a laugh. "Didn't do it for you." She reached down to stroke Markus. "You'd better be a fucking amazing dog, man. Don't think I'll be mentioning you to my parents when I ask for the cash."

Once he wuffed, there was a pause.

"So, um," Angelina began, "why *did* you do it?"

"For you, Angie." She gave an unhinged grin, reminding Angelina of her brother. "Now, I'm off to sort this money out. Please don't let Markus run off or anything like that."

TWENTY-ONE
TAKING OUT THE TRASH

"We could just do this tomorrow, Hobson."

"Nah, fuck it," Hobson said, taking the final short drop to the bottom of Peckham Rye station steps. Markus jumped along behind him. "We sort this out now, find a totally fresh case tomorrow. I'm thinkin' maybe a cheating husband or lost cat."

"Or we could tidy up the office," Choi muttered.

"The office is fine."

"There's a pile of old Social Awesome property the size of Tony's van covering a whole corner."

"And is it bothering anybody?"

Hobson beeped his way through the ticket barriers to get out into the hall, hearing Choi trail through another one to join him. "So, smells a lot nicer round here, doesn't it? Looked like a natural disaster earlier."

Choi shoved her Oyster card back into her pocket and peered out at the covered arcade outside the station. "You didn't even come inside. I almost choked."

"Just like we wanted, of course."

Markus started to whine as he scuttled around the floorspace, covering as wide a circle as his lead allowed. Everywhere he sniffed, some new horror sent him scampering away. The stench wasn't *completely* gone, it seemed.

Taking pity on the dog, Hobson made his way down the glorified alleyway, out to the high street itself. Shops were shuttering for the evening, the bearded brigade emerging onto the scene in greater force. Now he worked in East London, Hobson found himself treating them more and more as part of the landscape.

Still, seeing them sweeping into his old neighbourhood gave him pause. Gentrification closing in from all sides. Would've happened even if he never moved.

He looked up to the sky. It was dark, nearly nine, time for the evening fun to start. Choi reached the street at last, always taking a little longer.

"So," she said, "you really want to call off Operation S.O.S.? We don't need the money?"

"Nope. Carlton family kidnap cash meets my budget for the week and it's just…"

Hobson gestured up the road towards Jamie's Café. Lights shimmered warmly as people gathered around for the evening session, when it transformed into a glowing, chilled-out drinks venue. The dreadlocked guy who stopped Choi in the street earlier was outside having a beer. "This is what the place is now. New culture moving in, and bringing their street fundraisers with them."

"So you're rolling over and giving up? After nearly getting us all killed over a dog?"

"The dog mattered to me. This is bullshit." He chuckled. "Believe it or not, Choi, you almost had it right on your first day. If I want to make this detective thing work, I gotta at least do actual cases. Can't just have my mates pay me to chase kids off their fuckin' lawn. That shit ain't possible or worthwhile, really."

"Wow, cool." Choi smiled the widest he'd ever seen from her. "Does that mean I'm forgiven for letting Lettie take Markus?"

Hobson jerked into motion. "Let's get this over with. Benny and The Pimp are meeting us at Jamie's."

They made it three shops down the street, weaving around the rubbish as ever, before Choi piped up again.

"That Pimp guy makes me uncomfortable, Hobson."

"Yeah?"

"Yeah. The way he looks at me is nasty. If he *is* a pimp, are we *really* okay with that?"

"Well, I…" Hobson sighed. "Choi, don't get carried away just because I took a stand over Markus. I'm not a cop, I'm not here to smear justice all over Peckham."

She didn't emit any further words, merely a disappointed tut. Should never have told her she'd been right about anything. Hobson grinned.

Angelina felt a flash of extreme self-consciousness as she pushed the door to Jamie's Café open. It was full of young, skinny folk in tight shirts with thin beards, and she just wasn't that *with it*.

She was sixteen, of course – plenty of time to evolve. The café was dark, lit by shaded orange lights in the corners. They were new, rolled out for the all-cool evening shift. The space remained small, making its smooth nighttime mode all the more cosy. Behind the counter, Jamie bustled, selling coffees and beers to a languid groove.

Hobson entered behind her and the low lights darkened in his shadow. The whole café turned to investigate. Jamie looked up and scowled, but remained too penned in by customers to shoo them out.

Still, an atmosphere descended. Had people told each other about them flooding the station with trash? A sickening feeling ran through Angelina's bowels. What if Will turned against her too, because she was now out of style?

When Benny and The Pimp waved over from a corner, Angelina hurried over as fast as she could, grateful for the distraction. Their smart suits and, she had to admit, skin tones looked out of place in this crowd.

"Alright, chaps?" Hobson reached down and shook both their hands, before perching himself in one of Jamie's thin chairs. Markus shuffled along behind them and started sniffing the back of Angelina's knees.

"Ah, Mister Hobson, Miss Choi, hello. How are you?" Benny smiled. Even though she didn't approve of yelling about the Lord in the street, Angelina couldn't help but find him likable.

"I'm good, thanks," Angelina said, seating herself.

"Looking a bit of a mess there, missy," The Pimp chimed in, indicating the scuffing on her clothes. He all but licked his lips as he said it. She didn't reply, but made sure to catch her boss's eye.

"Okay," Hobson said. "Look, I'm afraid we've come to a decision about your case, and I ain't sure you'll like it."

The clients looked at each other. Angelina held her breath.

"I know I said we'd get rid of the chuggers for you, but I don't think we can. I think... they're just doing their jobs, you know? They're not some foreign parasite, just a sign of the way it's all going."

Long pause. The music rattled faster, determined to accentuate the silence.

The Pimp raised an eyebrow, Benny shrugged in response. A man with a cocktail in a coffee mug brushed past Hobson's shoulder.

At last, Benny spoke. "I can't pretend I'm not disappointed, Mister Hobson, but I appreciate your professional honesty."

Hobson nodded. "Least I can do, Benny."

The Pimp laughed. "Besides, everyone seems to fuckin' hate your approach anyway. You should hear the bitching in here tonight."

Something pinged in Angelina's head and she realised what she hadn't done all day.

She pulled out her phone, flicked up the Twitter app and ran a couple of searches. Managed to tune out Hobson's conciliatory chatter. Checked and double-checked the numbers.

"Hobson!" she squeaked, voice changing in ways she didn't intend. "We, um, there's an online backlash against the trash thing. We... Well, we've lost followers. Our brand's taken a beating, I think."

If that wasn't catastrophic enough, Jamie loomed up behind them, looking a lot less cuddly than he once had. The low light only added to his imposing presence.

"You two. Was I not clear enough last time about you not being welcome here?"

Hobson could probably take Jamie in a fight. The café owner was aggressively regular-sized and didn't seem to work out. Then again, he ran a business on Peckham high street, so must have a certain baseline of hardwearing toughness.

Although that wasn't as street-rough an activity as it used to be.

Anyway, Hobson told himself, he was only *allowing* Jamie to evict them from the café. Nonetheless, they all ended up outside – Hobson, Choi, Markus, Benny and The Pimp.

"Okay, you lot, enough," Jamie said, as he stood at the door supervising their exit. "I mean it this time. Some of us are trying to get on with our lives, we don't have time for childishly pranking a whole neighbourhood. And I've been on Twitter, I know people agree with me."

"We're sorry," Angelina leapt in immediately, "we were just trying to help, because they asked us and…"

"Choi," Hobson said. "Enough."

He held up a hand to Jamie. "Sorry about this, boss. We're gonna talk to everyone and get it fixed."

Jamie didn't go as far as smiling, but there was a small nod, maybe a tiny acknowledgment. Better than the squint-eyed stare of contempt he gave to The Pimp before heading back into his place.

Choi still looked red-eyed and distraught. For someone so calm when in control, she sure fell to pieces under pressure. Then again, her precious

Twitter following took a knock, so who knows what she might do?

While Hobson paused over how to deal with Choi's upset, The Pimp moved in, past Benny, to place a hand on her shoulder. Hobson wondered whether that was okay, or if he should've made any effort to comfort her.

He got his answer when she shouted out and hunched her shoulders back into her body, taking a few stumbled steps down the darkened street.

Benny looked lost, but Hobson was fine. He might be avoiding violence, but The Pimp wasn't a big guy. Pretty sure he could see this problem on its way with a muttered threat.

Before he could issue that stern warning though, a thin, dark-clothed shadow stepped into the middle. He slid around Benny and placed himself between Angelina and The Pimp. His legs were long, thin and brown-skinny-trousered, a red cardigan tight on his upper half.

"Will!" Choi said, suddenly thrilled.

"Lina, hi." He smiled, tucking his hair back out of his eyes. "You okay? I was just heading into Jamie's when I heard you yelling."

"Oh, yeah, I was just a little shocked, I mean…"

Will nodded, satisfied, and turned around to look at The Pimp. "I thought I told you to stop hanging around the building," he said, firmer than Hobson ever heard him before. Well, again, he must have *some* guts to be a doorman in this area.

"This ain't your building, Will," The Pimp said, smug as ever.

"Good point. Would you mind fucking off anyway?" He jabbed his thumb down the road. Hobson tensed up again.

The Pimp scowled at Will, then turned sideways at Benny.

"C'mon, dude," he said, stomping away into the darkness. "Let's go somewhere less full of hipsters. I bet this guy volunteers as a street fundraiser at the weekend."

Benny made a few apologetic noises to Choi, Hobson thought he picked out a *'so sorry about him'*, then they were gone.

Which left Hobson himself, he realised, standing around in the street with two kids who may or may not be dating. A few doors down from Jamie's now, the wind whipping around him, he felt his body fall slack with exhaustion. Time to go home.

"So, just gotta chat to a couple of the local shops, make sure they know not to throw more trash into the streets, then I reckon I'm off." Hobson started up the way. "You coming, Choi?"

She looked at Will. Will looked at her. Hobson looked at Markus.

"Um, I don't know," Will said, his floppy fringe conspiring with the stammer to make him look like a trendier Hugh Grant. "Did you say you were busy tonight, Angelina?"

"No, um," she gave him a small smile, "I think I'm free now."

"Yeah, I'm definitely leaving." Hobson stood firm. "See you tomorrow, Choi. Will, don't let her get mobbed by angry Twitter twatters or I'll feed you to my dog, okay?"

Markus did another *"Wuff!"*, then a few little pants. He didn't look ferocious or man-eating, but Will obligingly said *"Yes sir!"* nonetheless.

"So, um, hi. What are you up to?" Angelina said once Hobson was gone, painfully aware of the spilled beer smell lingering on her clothes. "If you already made other plans for tonight, we can always... I mean, I'm free tomorrow night."

"I said I'd meet some people in there." He gestured towards Jamie's Café. "But if you're saying you're now free again, we can go somewhere else for a bit."

"Yeah, okay," she said, before wondering if it was rude to pull him away from his friends.

"You alright?" Will looked down at her, eyes kind. He did not, to Angelina's pleasure, reach out for a sneaky shoulder grab.

"Yeah, sorry, I wasn't, um, I'm not always great with sudden changes of plan," Angelina babbled out.

"Okay, look, I've got people in there, so you won't be leaving me lonely, want to do tomorrow night like you said earlier?"

"Um," Angelina rubbed her temples. "That might be good, yes."

Other people were walking past them on the way in to Jamie's. Probably all thought Will was a grown-up looking after some upset kid.

"Okay. I'll message you tomorrow and we'll sort something out, yeah?"

The good thing about Will's constant chilled-out air: he never seemed annoyed about anything. Angelina felt a spike of guilt about booking a date on Friday night – *the most social night of the week* – but bashed it back down.

"That'd be nice, yes. Thank you."

"No problem. Want me to walk with you back up to the station?"

"Yes. Okay."

Hobson stopped dropping into local shops after the first two couple chased him out whilst yelling, ushering and pointing. Too scared they'd be seen talking to the man who stinkbombed the whole hood.

So he made his way back to the station and sank into a freezing metal bench, Markus at his feet. The train was ten minutes away, and he enjoyed just over five of them in a quiet, peaceful state of contemplation. Then he heard a humming, lilting, almost laughing sound wafting up the stairs. The accent was familiar.

"Choi?" he said, chuckling.

"Wuff?" said Markus.

Choi reached the top of the stairs, almost skipping along, before stopping dead and thudding to the ground when she saw Hobson. A level, businesslike tone reasserted itself by the time she formed a word. "Hobson? I thought you were going home?"

"Just missed a train. So, you seem pretty happy considering that must've been the shortest date in history."

Despite her face locking down in neutral, a smile slipped through. "Went okay. He already had plans so we're going out properly tomorrow."

"So I guess you'd like it if I didn't keep you busy all tomorrow night with some bloody awful horror-case?"

"If that's not too much trouble."

"Heh."

The train pulled up and the two of them leapt on board. Hobson was only going a few stops, but Choi had a long way to travel.

Other passengers stared resolutely downward around them. Phones, tablets, music players, cheap newspapers – no item was too boring to provide a focal point for the sober late night commuter.

But anyway: "So, your last day of work experience tomorrow, Choi. Anything you think you haven't learnt? Any requests? Aside from tidying the fuckin' office of course."

"Well, I think we need to look at getting our social media reputation back on track after this station-bombing disaster."

"Sounds like fun."

"Yeah," Choi laughed at his disdain, "I might post some cute pictures of Markus. They get a lot of traction online."

"So I've heard. You sure you wanna waste a day on that, considering you might not be here in two days?"

Choi looked up from her own phone-based stranger deterrent. "*Might* not be?"

He tried to read her expression, but nothing. "Well, it's the end of our official two weeks. Whether you stick around after that kinda depends on what we both want, doesn't it?"

"And do you? Want me to do anymore?"

He thought about it, crossed his fingers and lied. "Not decided yet. Do you?"

"I..." She looked out of the window for a second, and her eyes unfocused. This simple question took a lot of introspection.

"Not sure either," she said at last. "Think we did good work with Markus though. And even with the chuggers in the end."

She glanced down at the friendly animal, who was licking her ankles.

"Yeah," Hobson nodded. "Me too. And to think you were worried I'd punch them."

The train squeaked to a heavy stop, and Hobson looked out of the window. As he'd hoped, there was his local station, glowing in crappy darkness.

He gave her a small salute as the train hissed to a stop and snapped out: "See you tomorrow, anyway. Let me know what you decide, boss."

Her inscrutable face finally cracked into a smile as he leapt up, spun around a handrail and made his way to the door, trailing the dog's lead from one hand. The rest of the carriage tensed up, as if terrified he might swing into them.

Life was good, he thought to himself. Not *good* in the literal sense, but he felt less wracked with agony than yesterday. He almost called Ellie to tell her about it, but no. Mustn't brag at her whenever anything positive happened. Save it for when he wins *big*.

He did have a call to make, though, and may as well do it on the way home. Not as if he worried about people nicking his phone on the street – it was a piece of shit and he was a big guy with a big dog.

Hobson pulled the plastic brick out and dialled.

"Hey, Tony."

"Johnny, hi."

"Sorry about the other night. Shit got dark."

"Hardly the first time. So, I hear Twitter hates you guys. Something about shutting down a station?"

"Don't worry, we've got plans for tomorrow, we'll pull it back. But I need a favour, actually."

There was a definite sigh at that, but he still came back with: "What kind of favour?"

"You know that guy in the stupid hat and pimp costume who hung around my old office?"

"You mean The Pimp?"

"That's the fucker. Could you ask around about him, find out what his story is? Like, is he *really* a pimp, that sorta shit. Someone…" He sighed. "I had a query about it. Feels like I should know after all this time, I reckon."

"I suppose so, Johnny. You can owe me a dozen pints."

"Absolutely, mate. They can come out of the hundred you owe me. Night."

Hobson hung up. Definitely wouldn't be telling Choi about this until he had something solid. Now, whereabouts in his small flat would this large dog be sleeping?

As Angelina eased the front door closed, she held her breath. The hallway curved around the middle of her house, so she couldn't quite see all the way into the kitchen. The light was on, though, and the clank of plate on plate echoed through to confirm her Mum's presence.

Well, could be her Dad, but probably wasn't.

She placed her coat on the rack quickly – most of the manky scuffs and marks were on there or her trousers, her blouse not suffering too badly. The lights out here were still off – could she sneak upstairs before anyone noticed the mess? Admittedly, darkness wouldn't mask the underlying stench of lager.

Best try to act normal. "Hi Mum! I'm back!"

Still, her foot was poised on the bottom step, ready to go at the first sign of trouble.

"Angelina!" There was a clanging splash, and her mother appeared in the doorway, hair all askew. "You're back early."

"Oh yeah," Angelina nodded, "y'know. Sometimes we finish on time."

"So, I didn't see you on TV this time. No good cases?"

So their Peckham antisocial trash exploits hadn't made the news channels. Good. "Yeah, just a lost dog today."

"Oh, that's nice." For the first time, her Mum managed a sincere smile while talking about Angelina's job. "Did you find it?"

"Eventually, yeah. Turns out it was hiding."

"That's nice. And how was Zoë last night?"

"Oh, she's cool. Weirdly keen on spreadsheets. I'm gonna go get changed, if that's okay? Had to rustle around some messy gardens looking for this dog, got some mud on me."

Jesus, she was getting good at lying.

"Of course, I'll put some dinner on."

"Thanks Mum!"

Her thumping, sock-clad feet jerked into motion, whirling like a dynamo, but she only made it five or six steps when her Mum called her back, voice urgent and quick.

"Angelina!"

Halfway down the stairs, she gripped the shiny white bannister rails and leaned her face down against them.

"Yes, Mum?"

Her mother's cheeks turned red as she composed whatever this urgent question was, unable to keep it inside a moment longer. "So, are there any plans for your last day tomorrow?"

The tension drained out of Angelina's ankles, she sank until her knees hit the luxurious carpet of the stairs.

"I... I don't know. I'm not sure if I want it to be my last day."

"Really? Because you seemed to be having doubts about staying on Tuesday."

"Yeah. Hobson's not a perfect guy, but he's doing alright. The work is interesting. I don't think I want him to let me go."

"And have you told him that, dear?"

"Not in so many words."

"Well, then." Her Mum shrugged, suddenly cool, calm and turning away. "You know what I think, but it's up to you. There's only so much help I can give when I don't even know why you're there."

Angelina stayed sat on the stairs, left alone while a pizza went into the oven next door. She leaned her head back against a higher step and looked up.

Another three or four studio family portraits were spotted around the back wall, just far up enough to stop anyone shouldering them off their hooks. Usual poses: Angelina Choi and her parents against some mottled standard-blue backdrop. They loved that stuff.

Her parents weren't called Choi, of course. Her adoptive parents or her real ones, as far as she knew. The adults in the photo only looked like her if she squinted, and that hadn't felt like enough for a while. She always felt like a puzzle unsolved.

Well, even if Hobson wasn't a saint, her foot was in the door of detective work. Maybe it was time to wedge the rest of herself through.

HOBSON & CHOI
WILL RETURN
IN

CASE THREE: TRAPPED IN THE BARGAIN BASEMENT

CASE THREE
TRAPPED IN THE BARGAIN BASEMENT

BONUS STORY
INFERNAL ACCOUNTING

DAY ONE

My name is Gregory James. I used to be an accountant, and then I somehow became a supermarket manager. Sometimes, I think that whole chain of events was planned, on purpose, like they wanted some nobody to take this fall.

I'm getting ahead of myself, of course. The bad times only came after I was caught using Rush Recruitment – the temp agency who are really slave merchants. I hired them to staff the Anderson's megastore in Hackney with unpaid people. And why did I do that?

To make money, balance the books. To keep everyone happy, maybe get something for my effort at the end.

And what was my reward?

Rush said they'd try to sell my accountancy services. Seems they've wanted to move outside manual gruntwork for a while, and I'm a perfect opportunity. So I now live in a locked bedsit, rotting in the centre of some part of London I don't recognise. But I'm sure it's one I'd never usually visit.

The whole place is around the size of my old living room, enough space for a single bed, a cabinet and a few kitchen appliances, all broken. They're brown and stained, just like the walls. The light bulb is naked, windows smeared with brutal blackout paint to stop me getting any sunshine. Turn the light out and it's darker than you ever see in London.

Insects all over the browning-green carpet, holes forming and coming up at the corners. There's one dusty sofa but the TV is long gone. Assuming there ever was one.

It's like the evil twin of the flat I lived in when I first moved to London.

Got a tiny bathroom too – crusty toilet and mouldy bath with a rusty showerhead attached. At least they gave me a low-spec laptop with no internet to keep me entertained. They said I should feel lucky, the shelf-stacking scum don't get their own room *or* a computer.

Funnily enough, I don't feel special for being among the elite. Still, since I have the laptop, I thought I'd keep this diary, just tapped out in Notepad. Maybe someone will find it one day. Even if it's too late to help me, they'll *know*.

The first Rush guy I met was Rocky. That detective Hobson said he was a dickhead, but Hobson told them to lock me up, so who's the real dickhead? Rocky isn't much like me, but does that have to be a bad thing?

For example, Rocky said working at Rush was "top table, class A, premium export bants". I don't talk like that.

Nothing much else has happened. No food yet. Rocky dropped me here with some big goons to escort me to this room. The last thing he said to me: "Keep the peace, wankster – this is gonna be epic noise."

I still haven't worked out whether he called me a wanker. He left before I could ask. That was my first day. Typing this diary on the cruddy laptop just to distract from my hunger. Going to try sleeping now.

DAY TWO

Only the second entry in this diary no-one will read, and I'm already worrying it isn't any good. Like maybe the wretched old computer reads the raw text and thinks: "Wow, mate, you're boring."

At lunchtime, they gave me a pre-made chicken noodle snack from the Anderson's Budget Plus range. There isn't an Anderson's Budget line, if you were wondering – Budget *Plus* is the cheapest one we do. It's meant to trick people into thinking this isn't the lowest you can sink. We have better designed packaging than Tesco Value.

In short, it's a dirt-cheap Pot Noodle. It tastes like elastic bands, sand and polystyrene floating in dirty water. I don't recommend it, especially served by a grunting heavy. He took so long to hand it over, the boiling water went cold, so it looked and tasted like chilled vomit.

They didn't even give me the sauce sachet.

After that, I met Mister Gaines. He never tells me his first name. I introduced myself as "Greg," he shrugged it off.

Mister Gaines is tall and balding, wearing an M&S suit like I used to wear, getting chubby around the waist. Can relate to that too.

He says I'll be starting tomorrow. No details of exactly what I'll be doing. I asked, but he blanked the question and I didn't want to look stupid.

He left not long after. At least the process is moving forward, I suppose. Soon, I'll get back into a routine, and that'll be okay. Say what you will about Greg James, I'm good at following orders. Reliable, regular.

Once Rush Recruitment see that, maybe they'll ease off a little. Scrape the black paint off one of my windows, even.

DAY THREE

Already struggling to work out what day it is. Current best guess: Friday.

When Gaines knocked and said I should be ready to go in half an hour, I nearly jumped out of my skin. Only just settled down in time to shower before he was back. The water only goes up to lukewarm, I couldn't stop shaking.

Gaines ignored that, just growled "C'mon, bring your fuckin' laptop," and away we went. According to the clock on this useless machine, that was two in the morning. When I left my room though, it was bright outside, closer to ten or eleven.

We walked along the corridor, only saw a single tiny window every so often over the stairwells. The other front doors are as rigid and guarded as mine. This whole block serves as some kind of dorm-prison. I could hear talking or crying behind most of the other doors, different voices intermingled. I hated them a bit for their moaning. At least they had someone to whinge at.

At the bottom of the stairs, we entered a real room! With windows! A whole spectrum of sunlight! After two days in darkness, it almost blinded me. I had to bite down a shout. Didn't even mind the thin layer of scum over the scraped-down off-white walls.

The only object on the surprisingly clean table was a grey boxfile. Gaines opened it up, it was crammed with receipts, paperwork, scores of the same timeslips I'd signed off at Anderson's. All with 'Rush Recruitment' seared across them, in case I forgot why I was here. Sitting atop the mountain was a USB drive.

Gaines pointed at the scrappy pile and gave a slight nod, no smile.

"There you go," he said. Our accounts for this quarter. We let the paid accountant go yesterday after we signed you, so you'd better not fuck up. Get everything in order."

"And remember: we need to look dead fucking straight. Anyone looks at these and comes after us, we do you before the cops bash the door in. Yeah?"

Before I could try a sincere smile, he left, slamming the door behind him. I gulped, sat down and began trying to get the paperwork into the most legal state I could. Plugged the USB into my laptop which, despite its age, just about ran Excel. Opened up their spreadsheets.

The processor whirred and clunked whenever I tried to do anything complicated with formulae, but at least I had the basics. Maybe I'd ask for better equipment once I established my credibility and made them like me.

I worked solidly all day, until some goon loomed in. He waited for me to close up the laptop, prodded me along the corridor and stairs. As the sunlit windows disappeared into the distance, my hand almost reached out for them.

All I got to eat was another not-noodle, but at least I feel like I've done something today.

DAY SIX

They found some small mistake in the first day's work, so Gaines whipped me in the face with the butt of his knife. Said if I didn't shape up, I'd get the other end.

I think my cheek is bruising, but the mirror in my bathroom is too ruined with stains and cracks to be sure. It hurts, though.

Today, a small break in the routine. I hit a dead end in the accounts and needed to google a term. I almost didn't bother, just went with my best guess and hoped it worked, but I didn't want another smack round the face. The last one hadn't stopped throbbing yet.

Not to mention, I still want to prove I'm good, you know? They haven't found another mistake yet. Perhaps I show them I'm valuable, they bring the noodle snacks quicker from the kettle?

Maybe that's optimistic, I don't know.

So I asked to use the internet. Turns out, they really don't have it in this building. After all, none of the paid Rush staff live here, and they're hardly going to let the slave workers have Facebook, are they?

Instead, Gaines pulled out his smartphone. A pang of nauseous nostalgia shivered into me just seeing it. I feel like everyone is moving on without me. Maybe I always felt that way.

Gaines gave me his phone and said I could look up my "stupid fuckin' numbers problem". But I'd be supervised, to make sure I didn't do anything "unfortunate".

His phone screen was small, so Gaines placed it in my hands then leant over my shoulder. Pressed the edge of his knife into my neck.

My body shook so hard, I struggled to work the touchscreen. Couldn't stop thinking about the flesh of my adam's apple slitting against the blade. I felt a sharp pinch, then held dead still. A drop of blood ran down my breastbone, staining the already-disgusting clothes I'd worn since day one.

"C'mon," Gaines whispered, "get googling, Greg."

Autocorrect challenges me enough without this pressure, but I got the term typed out. The answer was one of the first few hits, thank Christ. I read it, I implemented it, I'm pretty sure the accounts are okay.

On my CV, it says I thrive under pressure. As I fell apart in front of my new boss, I couldn't stop thinking what an obvious lie that was.

As if he'd read my CV. As if that mattered.

DAY NINE

The error today was worse. I put a number in the wrong box, then a string of bad calculations followed. I'm not claiming to be some accounting savant – I imagine my life would be better if I were. Probably wouldn't have left the profession to try mid-level management. Still, I hoped I was above such basic screw-ups.

And that's when things went awful. I got a slap around the face with the knife handle from Gaines, then a through bashing around the ribs from a bigger guy. Felt one of the bones give in, just crunch away.

They said I was lucky they couldn't mess up my

face too much right now, but if I started to seem incompetent, that wouldn't be a problem.

Can't shake the feeling someone pissed in my budget noodle snack. At least they still gave it to me, though.

It was just the taste, a lingering sourness.

The laptop says it's Thursday, but I think it might be lying.

DAY TWELVE

When we got back from that sunny room downstairs today, I saw a dry-cleaning bag left on my bed. At first, I assumed it would be a strait jacket or something else terrible.

But no, it was a suit, fresh and pressed. New clothes at last! The current ones were starting to rot. Not an amazing suit – rough and cheap, obvious seams – but I've seen work colleagues turn up in worse.

Next to it was a small stack of plain, featureless t-shirts. They were thin and unsatisfying to touch, but still better than nudity. Plus cheap jeans, possibly Anderson's Budget Plus again. Couldn't be sure, all labels were cut away.

Tears began in my eyes as I turned to face Gaines. All I said was: "Thank you."

"Yeah, don't cum just yet." Gaines snorted. "This ain't no Christmas present, you got a gig. Means we gotta polish the turd a bit."

"Oh," I said.

"There's an electric razor on your bedside table too," he continued, and I rushed over to inspect it like a kid on Christmas morning. "If you ain't looking like a presentable worker by morning, there will be consequences. Y'understand?"

"Don't worry, Mister Gaines, I understand."

"Would hope so, it's dead simple and you're meant to be clever. And the same rule every day after that, yeah? None of this complacency bullshit."

"Of course."

"Good." Gaines nodded and turned to leave, before looking back, reaching into his suit jacket. Despite everything he'd said so far, I still flinched away. Half-expected him to pull out a taser and shock me for the sake of it, but instead it was a tiny circular metal pot.

"Shoe polish," he said as he threw it over. "Your feet look like you've been living in a swamp. Clean them. No excuses. Use your filthy old clothes as a rag."

He threw the polish at me and left, slamming the door behind him.

And dinner this evening: microwave chicken tikka! Every mouthful of meat and sauce felt like it was bringing me back to life, bursting with flavour that spread right out to my fingertips. With no-one there to judge me, I licked the plastic compartment clean, then commenced getting ready for work the next day.

To be honest, my bowels were unsettled after going from bland nothingness to curry, but the rumbling nausea was worth it.

Assuming this isn't an elaborate trick, tomorrow I leave the building! See other people! Have a shave, clean my shoes, whistle as I go to work.

I can't wait. So happy they're letting me do this. Mustn't get anything wrong. Best go to bed now rather than typing anymore.

DAY THIRTEEN

Even though today was my first day of freedom, it started on a tense note. Gaines woke me at six to lay down the rules.

Most of them are what you'd expect. For example: do not, under any circumstances, tell anyone anything about Rush Recruitment. Your name is Jason Williams, here's basic paperwork for that identity, *do not* tell anyone who you really are.

You'll get a packed lunch every day, no money. If a colleague suggests socialising after work, even if they're offering to pay, *do not* say yes.

The office is twenty minutes walk away, you will not get an oyster card or any other way of using public transport. You're expected back by six thirty at the absolute latest. You also get a cheap prepaid mobile to let them know of unavoidable problems.

Gaines ran over all that and more, at great length and with all the swearing and implied threats you'd expect. Glared, punched the bedside table, pointed at stuff, described the horrible things he'd do if I made a single mistake.

He couldn't destroy my good mood, though. In fact, my constant smiling annoyed him more. But I was going *outside*, and I didn't care if grinning about it made me look like an idiot.

I turned as I left, just to look at the place I'd lived in for the last two weeks. I imagined some military prison, but it was just a block, really. Grey, dulled textures, nothing special. I'd never have focused my eyes on it while passing.

But anyway, I was off to work! Walking! I made damn sure I whistled. The sun started up, soon it was going to burn. I hurried to work in my suit, keen to get the jacket off before I sweated through my shirt. Considering how much Gaines wanted me to make a good impression, wouldn't do to turn up with enormous armpit stains.

I looked down at the crumpled online map printout Gaines shoved into my hand earlier. I was there. Outside a circular brick building, rented office space shining out on all sides. Somewhere inside this capitalist donut was my new employer.

Westman & Cooper. Not a firm I'd heard of, but what was I expecting?

So in I went, nodded to the receptionist and gulped like a fish.

"Hello," said the receptionist. "Can I help?"

He was a nobody in a suit, everything about him bland. But he was a person talking to me.

"Hi," I said, straining for normality through a massive grin, "I'm a temp at Westman & Cooper, starting today?"

"Ah, I see," he reached for his phone. "Name?"

"Jason Williams," I said, trying to sound natural.

"Uh-huh, thanks, wait over there."

He pointed over to some beaten brown leather chairs and I sat down. He called up the firm and, before I even got comfortable, my new boss bounded down.

He skipped through the door, hand already out there for the shake. He was short, stocky and friendly, smile sat on his face like it lived there. A bit older than me, like a friendly uncle. Thinning brown-grey hair and a firm grip.

"Mr Williams?" He smiled. "I'm Jack Westman, one of the partners here, how are you doing?"

"Fine, thanks." I grinned. "Good, even. You?"

"Oh, you know!" Big affected string of nods, an endearing *just-the-way-it-goes* laugh. "Busy busy busy, but that's why you're here, isn't it son?"

"Yeah, definitely!" I said, matching his enthusiasm beat for beat.

Westman pointed towards the next door, and behind there was the lift. Before long, I was whisked up to their office.

The lift was slow, but they'd fashioned the back panel out of glass so I could see the central courtyard. It really was a donut, right down to the hole in the middle. People sat on benches in the sunshine. I vowed to try that myself before today ended, and I did just that.

But first, I met the other partner in the company. I entered the office, it was a large space, especially considering only two of them worked here. The other one was Alex Cooper – big smiles, short brown hair, around the same age and height as Westman, very friendly. Almost too friendly, in fact – not flirty, just asked a lot of questions.

Cooper asked me how I was, if I'd come far, what my place was like, how I liked my coffee. After one conversation, I think she knew me better than my mother.

Of course, my mother knew nothing about the fictional studio flat I improvised for Jason Williams. It was small, cosy, the bed tucked into a little alcove, sometimes the neighbours were a tad loud.

Westman and Cooper wore matching wedding rings, I noted. There was no obvious public affection, but they seemed comfortable with each other.

I could've just asked if they were married, considering how much they'd interrogated me, but I never got round to it.

Instead, probably rather abruptly, I brought the chummy introductions to an end and asked what they needed me to do. Cooper looked wounded, but Westman nodded, said something about me being a "good worker" and found some spreadsheets to start on.

Then they directed me to the third desk in the room, close to the front door, cleared specially.

And there I sat all day, making occasional small talk, drinking machine coffee. Once, I made a mistake in a formula, just because I could. Sat outside for lunch, Cooper talking at me about plans for her front garden.

It was amazing. Even the terse debrief and noodle snack on my return couldn't bring me down. Maybe because they *did* give me the sauce sachet this time.

DAY FIFTEEN

Third day at Westman & Cooper, and I think it's going well. I didn't write yesterday because, I don't know diary, sometimes I feel like you're encouraging me to wallow.

I'm hardly the first person in the world to live alone, after all. Now I have a proper day job with friendly colleagues, do I *need* you? I've constructed a whole flat, neighbours, family and life for Jason Williams. Yesterday, after I came home, I lay down on my bed for an hour and imagined I was him.

Jason grew up in Wolverhampton, went to the local comprehensive. Excelled at maths, went to do a degree in it. Most likely, he'd be at the top of a big corporate accountancy firm by now, if not for going off the rails at uni and repeating a couple of years.

But at least he'd joined a band, gone travelling around Europe, had some wild times, finally decided to return and work on a career.

You should hear about his adventures, diary. I've already got into the habit of planning my anecdotes for the next day. Once, he went to Oktoberfest in Munich, got drunk and had a threesome with a backpacker and a woman in lederhosen. (I've never been to Germany.)

He never did anything stupid like trying to manage a supermarket. When Jason Williams made decisions, he chose the exciting ones and redeemed himself later.

Because there was always time. It was never too late.

I threw up most of today's noodle snack. Those sandwiches they give me for lunch are made of cardboard. I nearly screamed with relief when Cooper handed me a spare cheese baguette left over from a client meeting, then wondered if there was any way Rush could find out.

Covered for my over-excitement and panic by telling her it reminded me of a dairy farmer I'd almost married in Switzerland one summer.

DAY SEVENTEEN

Today was Friday. For a while, I lost track of the days, but now I'm back in a regular office job, each part of the week has its distinct ebb and flow again.

The slow sigh of Wednesday, gentle gasp of Thursday and, at last, the frenzied anticipation of Friday, the determination to get spreadsheets done so you can enjoy the weekend without worrying. I missed each and every one of them.

Of course, I'm a temp, so I don't *need* to care about my work, but I still do. Westman and Cooper are good people, I don't want to let them down. Don't want them to stop employing me either. God knows what workhouse nightmare Rush might find for me instead.

I bashed out of a load of figures, didn't let myself make any mistakes. They took me out for lunch at a nearby pizza place – I decided that didn't counteract any of the rules Gaines set out. Also: I still can't refuse food, I think my skin is starting to turn yellow.

Sometimes, I worry that my job here is professional third wheel, but Westman and Cooper aren't overt about being a couple. They held hands on the way back to the office from lunch, but still made conversation.

At the end of the day, they asked if I wanted to grab a drink with them in a nearby pub – that *was* explicitly against the Rush rules. It wouldn't be just the three of us, they stressed. Other people from the building were always there too, my chance to meet everyone. They'd even pay for a few drinks if I was worried about money.

And we weren't in mainland Europe, they said with a wink, so we wouldn't bump into any of my exes. The blood rushed to my face and I almost screamed at them for believing such obvious bullshit.

Instead, I mumbled an excuse and shuffled away back home. I still felt a little tug, slight Friday feeling. I wondered if maybe Rush would give me a better dinner than usual, let us watch some TV even.

None of that happened. But the mere feeling filled me with this real glee.

DAY EIGHTEEN

When Gaines woke me around eight in the morning on Saturday, I was almost stupid enough to feel surprised. Nearly lulled into believing a traditional full-time job meant weekends off.

Since starting the Westman & Cooper assignment, I manage my own waking-up times using the alarm on that cheap burn-off mobile. No-one told me I needed to set one for today.

Instead, my wake-up call came in the form of thudding and yelling from outside: "Greg! Wake up! You gotta finish all our paperwork today and tomorrow so you can go back to work Monday!"

I could've cried. My arms wouldn't move.

Gaines continued: "Don't make me come in there, Greg. If you get enough done, we might let you have some food today."

So I got up, pulled jeans and a thin t-shirt on and let them haul me to that tiny room downstairs. Put the laptop down on the table. The USB stick, payslips and forms waited there for me.

Gaines patted me on the shoulder and laid down the law: "Good fuckin' Saturday, Greg. If it makes you work any faster, this is all you got for the whole weekend. Any time left after this, you can have to yourself – unless you mess up, of course. Get to it."

Sadly, I worked harder than ever. Even faster than I had during the week for Westman & Cooper.

I'm starting to realise: I'm not even that good an accountant. I couldn't tell you how many times I needed to ask for help and couldn't. Had to do another knife-to-throat googling at one point.

But I made it. I got to the end. I ran over and asked Gaines if I could work late, to make sure I finished that last pile. I cheered when I pulled back from the desk, before they told me to shut up.

It was getting dark outside, but I couldn't stop smiling. Even smirked as I lay still all evening. I wish I'd felt this good about my fully-legal tasks in a supportive environment.

DAY NINETEEN

I should've left some work for today. At least I'd have left the room for a while.

No human contact except a brief nod from the grunty man who brings the food. They gave me overcooked pasta for dinner rather than the usual noodles, I suppose – although with no sauce, it was almost worse.

Stared at the wall. Looked at the mobile phone they gave me, wondering if I could call the police – call *anyone* to get me the fuck out of here. Yes, Rush would kill me for that, but if I shut them down – even just exposed this one section of their business – it would be worthwhile, wouldn't it?

Looked at the sharp, broken edges of the scummy wardrobe, imagining opening up my wrists and letting this awful life leak away.

Couldn't do either. Too scared.

The worst thing to realise about yourself, I think, is that you don't have any principles. Nothing is important enough to take a risk. You just sit, hoping someone else changes it for you.

Maybe this is why I've never had a substantial relationship, barely any sex. Not like Jason Williams. He was a player. Must be good to be him.

Work tomorrow. Might stay in the office at lunchtime and look at porn on the internet.

DAY TWENTY-THREE

It's Thursday, so yes, I've been away from you for a while. To be honest, I've got out of the diary habit, because this life is repetitive.

I go to work, Westman and Cooper are nice. I go back to the Rush building, Gaines is horrible.

I cry in bed and go to work in the morning. Couple of nights ago, I crashed out when I got home. Sobbed on the floor for ages without changing out of my work clothes. They ended up a crumpled, tear-stained mess, and I wasn't scheduled for a new set the next day.

Since I'd already ruined the suit, Gaines and his friends kicked me around the ribs until blood trailed up my shirt.

Thinking back about it now, isn't blood impossible to get out? So they've turned the suit from stained to a write-off?

Anyway. I went to work, not noticing or remembering anything on the way. Someone exiting the tube nearly shoved me into the road for not looking where I was going.

But I made it in the end. Strolled into the office, exchanged relaxed greetings with Westman. Cooper asked me how the meal with my parents went last night. I lied a lot and got on with work.

Don't go out at lunchtime. Don't do much at all.

Can't feel my head at times.

An hour before the end of the day, Westman comes over with his serious face on.

"So, Jason, we've enjoyed having you here the last couple of weeks. I was wondering if you've given much consideration to the future?"

"What do you mean, Jack?"

"Well, we've had a couple of temps through and we haven't enjoyed having any of them around as much as you. Are you interested in coming on board permanently?"

"Permanently? As in work for you?"

"Well, yes." Westman smiled, like he was welcoming me into the family. "Rush give us a ridiculous rate on you, I'm honestly not sure how you survive. Your starting salary wouldn't be amazing, but definitely a step up."

"Wow. This is so nice of you."

I was certain *this* would be against Rush's rules. I couldn't take the risk. They would never let me go. It wasn't worth it. At the least, I should go and ask their permission before saying yes.

Best make something up. Tell them I need time to think.

"Yes," I say. "Of course, I'd love to."

They seem delighted, agree to get the paperwork ready for tomorrow, and I went back to let Rush know.

Gaines laughed, told me not to be so fucking stupid and got one of his people to smash the two smallest toes on my right foot with a wooden mallet. That end of my sock looks like a bag of crushed cherries. A few more quick punches, then back into my room.

It's five in the morning. I haven't moved for hours.

Have to go to work soon.

DAY TWENTY-FOUR

Entered the donut today, under strict instructions from Gaines not to hobble or limp. That's what we call it, the donut. Those of us who work there. We.

Waved to the dull receptionist, who looked depressed to see me as ever. Westman refers to him as "Lurch", which is obvious but funny. He has a huge forehead, you see.

As the lift hissed upwards, I saw the sun bursting over the central garden and I think a tear sprang out. Only just wiped it off in time.

Still couldn't quite get past Cooper.

"Hi, Jason," she cooed as soon as I entered. "What's wrong? You look a bit down."

"I, um, yeah."

"Is there a problem?"

I almost burst into a proper sob. Not quite, though.

"Yeah, I'm afraid I need to talk to you both."

Narrowing her eyes, she went to get Westman.

Soon enough, we all sat around the table in their cluttered meeting area.

"Hi, guys, so," I said, trying to smile, "thanks for the opportunity. But I've had time to think overnight and I think I'll have to turn it down.

"Why?" Westman looked aghast. "Has someone else made an offer?"

"No, I just…" I gulped. Gaines told me to come up with a reason, and after only half an hour's thought, I had it. I've become so good at playing Jason.

"I don't wanna be tied down, you know?" Fresh smile. "Don't want to commit too much, have to be free to go."

"Ah, of course." Despite his disappointment, a twinkle sprang to Westman's eyes. "We understand, young man. Don't want to keep Europe waiting."

Definitely saw Cooper throw her husband a glare.

Hard to blame him, though. The life of Jason Williams sounded fun.

The rest of the day felt odd. Like the Westman-Coopers and I were in a relationship – they'd proposed, I'd turned them down. Now we hung around, wondering where it was all going.

Even though it was Friday, they didn't invite me out for a drink. Just waved and headed away. Gaines and the Rush people didn't react much when I got back, either. Just waved me into my room, the usual dinner arrived at the usual time.

I didn't eat it. Couldn't move from my bed once I lay down. Writing to you is the only thing I've done all evening, diary, and you don't exist. Maybe I should have given you a name.

DAY TWENTY-NINE
I think I'm only writing because it's been a while, to be honest. Five days, the longest I've gone without a diary entry since I arrived. Nothing improved since I turned down the job offer on Friday. Westman not as friendly, Cooper barely interested in my anecdotes, Gaines less inclined to give me a break.

Not only did he make me do the Rush accounts on Saturday and Sunday, he gave me a mop and cleaning equipment and told me to scrub my room. Apparently if the accounts weren't done *and* my bedsit clean, he would "make me wish I'd never been fucking born."

The bedsit is coated in baked-on scabby filth, of course. Cleaning it would be impossible. But I did my best, they laughed and at least didn't hit me anymore.

For the next few days, I worked and went home and ate barely-there tissue paper sandwiches and limped and stared. I wouldn't say I'm hearing voices, but I do talk to them.

I used to want a routine I could rely on. People who would always be there. Maybe now I've got it.

At work one day, I logged onto my old Greg James Facebook account for the first time in a month. Loads of messages, didn't read any. Felt like I was snooping into the life of a stranger. I could've messaged anyone and told them where I was, but what could they do?

Still throwing up occasionally. Blacked out on the toilet earlier. I don't know.

Stopped typing for a second there, because Gaines popped in to say he'd found mistakes in the Rush accounts I did at the weekend. Smashed me around the face with the hilt of his knife, same as usual.

Just another week. I keep telling myself this isn't a normal life. But that isn't how I feel, you know?

DAY THIRTY-ONE

Had another sit-down with Westman today. No indulgent cheer this time. Just the firm horizontal mouth of grim necessity.

Apparently I'd made a few mistakes in my work this last week. In light of me turning down the job offer, they felt it best to try some other temps. Keep moving until they found the right individual to forge a long-term career with the company.

They hoped I wouldn't take it personally. Wished me the best in all my future endeavours.

I'd fired people before. I hated it, but I was manager, I didn't have a choice. They were nobodies anyway, shelf-stackers. People I'd only seen in passing until the time came to cut them loose.

And that was how he came across. Like I was nobody.

Then I went home. Gaines told me I'd ruined a lucrative contract for them. Since they didn't have many contacts in the accountancy industry, they'd struggle to find me anything new for Monday. Meant it didn't matter so much if they hit me in the face.

As I dabbed at my black eye with rough one-ply toilet roll and spat blood into the sink back in my room, I wondered what happened next. Don't remember going to bed. Not sure I'll remember typing this. My skin really looks wrong.

DAY THIRTY-TWO

I only made it an hour into Rush's accounts today when Gaines rushed back into the room and snatched the paperwork away from me. Asked if I was taking the piss. Slapped me, obviously.

It made sense, I think.

The room was flickering and I could smell burning. Then I ended up back in my bed and I don't remember how I got there. Retched a few times but nothing came up.

I heard a voice and it was either Westman or my father, and he said: "Greg, you're not tried hard enough."

And I said *"What else could I have done?"*, but he didn't dignify it with an answer.

I think I saw someone else as well, maybe another person? Another worker? But the door never unlocked, so how could it be?

She was skeleton-thin, in torn clothes. To be honest, maybe I just saw her on TV. Comic Relief or some other charity TV marathon I watched but never donated to.

Something isn't right. She's standing in the corner but I'm just writing this and ignoring her. Can you see her, diary?

I'm not sure anyone can.

She looks like a slave from television. She looks beaten. I think my eye is infected. I think I'm going to die. I've been too scared to take my shoe off and look at my toes ever since they hit them with that hammer. So I sleep in the shoes, my feet feel all warm and funny. Something sticky leaking through the leather.

I want to hate Hobson for sending me here, but I can't.

She doesn't look as bad as me, I'm not sure anyone does. She has this defiance in her eye and I know I don't.

The sharp splinters on the side of the wardrobe don't look so scary now. Have I eaten for the last two days?

I'm going to stop now. I think I need to.

DAY THIRTY-SIX

It might be thirty-seven or thirty-five. Might be forty.

Gaines came back today. He said Rush was shutting down the accountancy division. They tried, I failed.

I'd made too many mistakes, in both the last week at Westman & Cooper and my final go at Rush's own accounts. They suspected Rush's approach to employment isn't compatible with professional careers.

Not to mention: he'd read my diary and decided I was "coming fucking unglued".

At last, he asked what I had to say to that. I kept lying in the same foetal position I'd assumed as he entered.

I'd eaten a few meals in recent days but that was about all I'd done. I don't want to die, you see, but nor do I want to do anything else.

Gaines stormed off after a while, but at least he didn't hit me. I was getting the hang of this now.

Considering I now know he reads this, you might ask why I'm continuing it.

You'd have a point. Hello, Mister Gaines.

DAY FORTY

Today, I got woken up by Gaines as ever, given new jeans and plain grey t-shirt. At first, I thought they'd be too small, but no, it was fine. I've lost a lot of weight while living here.

I stepped out, twitching into the sun. The white light opened up to embrace me. In front of me was a crowd of others. Dozens of accents, races, heights. These were *them*, I realised. My Rush Recruitment colleagues.

Not one of them looked anything like the woman from my room the other day.

Once everyone was there, we marched in small groups down the road to a branch of a well-known supermarket, one of my competitors from the old Anderson's days. I chatted, very quietly in short phrases, to a woman on the way down. She seemed sad but friendly enough.

Once we arrived at the supermarket, we were put to work. They gave me a uniform – everyone else already had one in a transparent carrier bag – and showed me how to stack shelves. They liked how quickly I understood their internal systems.

People smiled, it didn't hurt and there were others with me. I still twitched sometimes, my head screamed, but still. Even though I wasn't special, wasn't the only man of my kind on the Rush Recruitment books anymore, I felt better than I had in ages.

We all talked. I swiped some out-of-date food from the supermarket with help from a new colleague.

It was so okay, I barely feel the need to write this diary entry, to be honest. Maybe things will be alright. Anyway, they're taking the laptop away now I'm going into the general workforce, so I won't have any choice.

Thank you for everything. I don't know if I'd have made it here without you.

ACKNOWLEDGEMENTS

The logical place to start the *Book Two* acknowledgements is to thank everyone who bought *The Girl Who Tweeted Wolf*, thus empowering me to do it all over again. Double-plus-thanks to those who reviewed either book anywhere, regardless of comments/rating – cheers for taking the time!

Since the first book, we've become the biggest story ever on JukePop Serials, won their biannual prize and wrapped up the webserial with its one-hundredth chapter. Even if it dies now, *Hobson & Choi* has been a stunning achievement for me, and I couldn't have done it without the many lovely readers out there. Much obliged.

As before, Design For Writers (cover design), BubbleCow (edits) and The Big Green Bookshop Writing Group (therapy) were crucial to getting this book done. I'd also like to thank Jim from YA Yeah Yeah for regular support, PR mastermind Faye Rogers for promotional assistance and the many nice folk of the Super Relaxed Fantasy Club for making publishing books (even non-fantasy ones) seem surprisingly real, plausible and human.

And lastly, again, Leanne, for fielding my questions and worries about areas she is not an expert in with impressive levels of authority.

ABOUT THE AUTHOR

Nick Bryan is a London-based writer of genre fiction, usually with some blackly comic twist. As well as the detective saga *Hobson & Choi*, he is also working on a novel about the real implications of deals with the devil and has stories in several anthologies.

More details on his other work and news on future *Hobson & Choi* releases can be found on his blog at **NickBryan.com** or on Twitter as **@NickMB.** Both are updated with perfect and reasonable regularity.

Subscribe to his mailing list using the form in the sidebar of **NickBryan.com** to get news first *and* an all-new free *Hobson & Choi* short story immediately!

When not reading or writing books, Nick Bryan enjoys racquet sports, comics and a nice white beer.

Printed in Great Britain
by Amazon